A PROBLEM IN PAXTON PARK

A PAXTON PARK MYSTERY BOOK 5

J. A. WHITING

To hear about new books and book sales, please sign up for my mailing list at:

www.jawhitingbooks.com

❁ Created with Vellum

For my family with love

W ith her Calico cat, Justice, curled up next to her, Shelly Taylor slept in her comfortable bed in the bungalow she rented in the mountain resort town of Paxton Park, Massachusetts. It was a clear night in late May with the stars sparkling high in the sky and the nearly-full moon's light battling the darkness.

Sound asleep, Shelly turned over and a dream began to play in her mind.

She and her friend and neighbor, Juliet, ran together along the forest trails past the towering pines that lined the paths, their feet stepping into golden pools of dappled sunlight as they moved at a quick pace through the woods at the base of the mountains. Because it was only a dream, Shelly wasn't winded at all and she felt like she could run for miles and miles without tiring and without the slight ache in her leg that was always present when she ran.

Finally, the young women slowed to a walk and headed down the trail to where it ended at a large park.

A slender woman with soft brown hair falling just below her shoulders stood at the end of the trail watching Shelly and her friend approach, and when Shelly saw her, her heart flooded with joy.

Lauren. Her twin sister.

Just as Shelly was about to hurry to her, Lauren lifted her hand, her index finger in the air, urging Shelly to wait a moment.

Lauren turned and glanced at the walkway near the trees that led away from the woods and into the park, and when Lauren looked back at her sister, she gave Shelly a warning look, and slowly, slowly, she disappeared.

Shelly walked gingerly to the end of the path. She thought she saw something on the ground, but before she could investigate, a loud bang and a flash went off in her head.

Waking suddenly from the dream, Shelly bolted

upright in her bed and blinked as she looked around the bedroom feeling disoriented and shaken.

Her clock radio was on the floor, the alarm honking like a fog horn while Justice sat on the side table in the clock's usual place staring at the young woman.

Shelly's light brown hair tumbled over her shoulders as she reached down to turn off the bleating alarm and she asked the cat, "Did you knock the clock off the table when you jumped up there?" Noticing the time, she said, "Oh, gosh. I'm going to be late. Has this thing been going off for fifteen minutes and I didn't even hear it?"

Jumping out of bed and hurrying to get dressed, she looked at the Calico with a smile. "That's why you knocked it off the table. Thanks for waking me, Justice."

SHELLY'S NEIGHBOR, Juliet, was dressed in a t-shirt, bike shorts, and light jacket and was pumping the tires on her bicycle when Shelly dashed out of the house.

"Morning, sleepy head," Juliet said. "I was about

to bang on your door. I checked your tires already. We're all set."

Shelly thanked her friend. "I overslept by fifteen minutes. It would have been longer, but Justice knocked the clock-alarm off the table because I didn't wake up when it went off."

"Good thing the cat is on the ball," Juliet grinned. "Otherwise, I would have left without you."

The young women put on their helmets, rode down the lane to the town's Main Street, and took a left towards the resort where they would leave their bikes while they ran three miles on the trails before work. The sun had just lifted over the horizon and was painting the sky with pinks and lavenders and various shades of blue.

"I saw Lauren in my dream last night," Shelly told her friend as they rode along the street in the bike lane.

Juliet took a quick glance at Shelly. "Did you? It's been a while. Is anything wrong?"

"I don't think so. Well, I'm not sure. In the dream, you and I were running through the woods. Lauren was at the end of the trail waiting for us. She gestured for me to move slowly."

"Why did she?" Juliet asked.

"I woke up before I could find out."

The two sisters had lived and worked in Boston before a terrible car accident took Lauren's life and left Shelly with serious injuries and a long, painful recovery. A talented baker, Shelly had saved and scrimped and was about to purchase a bakery in downtown Boston when fate caused a change of plans. Unable to work during her months-long rehabilitation, Shelly had to use her savings to support herself which put an end to her dream of buying her own bakery ... at least until the day she was able to replenish her savings. Shelly applied for and was offered a part-time job as a baker at the resort in western Massachusetts so she left the city and moved to the beautiful mountain town of Paxton Park.

Ever since the accident, Lauren occasionally appeared in her sister's dreams, and when she did, it was usually to give clues or information about a particular crime that had occurred in the area.

Juliet's sister, Jayne 'Jay' Landers-Smyth, was a veteran police officer in town who encouraged Shelly to take her sister's dream-visits seriously believing that Shelly's mind used the appearance of Lauren to point out something important she'd ignored or overlooked during her waking hours ...

things that very often ended up being key to solving several criminal cases.

"So did your sister just drop in to say hello?" Juliet asked as they rode onto the resort's extensive grounds past lawns, a lake, rental condos, a hotel, several restaurants, and a promenade of high-end shops.

"I hope so," Shelly said in a soft voice, dismounting from her bicycle and locking it into the bike rack outside the employees' building.

They took their helmets inside to leave in their lockers and then headed out to run on the paths and trails that wound around the base of the mountain.

"Nothing has happened in town since winter," Juliet said as they started their run. "Everything's been quiet for months. No crimes, no misdemeanors, no trouble. Was Lauren's appearance in your dream a warning that the quiet time is about to end?"

"I like it quiet so I hope not." Shelly's breathing started to even out as she began to fall into her jogging rhythm.

"Are you worried?" Juliet asked.

"It was only a dream." Shelly said, a pulse of anxiety moving through her as she and Juliet ran along the trails side-by-side.

"How many times have I heard that?" Juliet reminded her friend.

Shelly ignored the question and moved the conversation to the early spring weather, what was going on around the resort, and their plans to go out for dinner together with their boyfriends on the weekend.

During the last quarter-mile of the run, Shelly's leg began to stiffen and ache, but she pushed through it and completed the planned three miles. When she slowed to a walk to cool down, she moved with a slight limp which was an ever-present and unpleasant reminder of the car crash.

The early morning sun was slightly higher in the sky and the warming air felt good against Shelly's sweaty skin as they headed down the trail to the park where they would loop around and head back to the employees' building to shower, change, and head out to start their workday at the resort.

Juliet was talking about an adventure hike she would be leading the next day explaining that so many tourists had signed up for it, they were scrambling to find another guide to go along.

"More guests are visiting the resort earlier in the year. Management must be very pleased," Shelly said.

Stepping out of the woods onto the walkway that led through the park, a wave of nervousness began to pulse over Shelly's skin causing her heart rate to speed up. She looked from one side of the space to the other. A few people were walking their dogs, a couple strolled hand-in-hand, a young man jogged near the playing fields, and several people sat on the benches that were set here and there along the walkways.

Shelly tried to shake off her unease by taking slow, deep breaths, but the feeling lingered and picked at her. Taking a look to the tree line, she halted abruptly.

For a few moments, Juliet didn't notice that her friend had stopped and then she realized she was walking alone. Turning around, she saw Shelly staring off to a point near the trees. "What is it?" she asked warily.

"There." Shelly gestured. "What's that in the grass?"

Juliet looked to where her friend's gaze was focused. "Is someone asleep near the trees?"

When Shelly started across the grass, Juliet hurried to catch up to her.

"Wait." Juliet gripped her friend's arm. "Hold up."

Shelly asked, "Is it...?" And then she let her voice trail off.

They moved a little closer, and then stopped short.

"Oh, no." Shelly took a couple of more steps and crouched down. A gasp escaped her throat when she saw more clearly what was before her ... a man on his side, half on the walkway, half in the grass, facing away from them towards the trees.

"There's blood," Shelly said in a shaky voice. "His head." She turned away and pulled her phone from her short's pocket. "I'll call for an ambulance. You should call Jay. Tell her there's a problem."

"I think it's too late for an ambulance, but you better call anyway." Juliet's eyes were pinned on the man in front of them, and as she pressed on her phone to make the call to her sister, she said to her friend, "Now we know why Lauren was in your dream last night."

Shelly's stomach tightened as she knelt beside the man to feel for a pulse and it took all of her strength not to become ill.

2

Three people stopped within minutes of one another when they noticed Shelly and Juliet standing by the body.

A young man in his mid-twenties was jogging up the slight incline and did a double-take when he saw the man on his side on the grass. When he offered to help, Juliet told him she'd called for emergency assistance and that the unconscious man didn't seem to have a pulse.

A tall, very slender, older man on his way to work at the town utility company hurried over to see if there was anything he could do and a woman in her mid-forties who was walking to her job as a receptionist at the hospital saw the people standing over the man on the ground and offered to help until she saw the head injury the man had sustained. She stepped back and turned away, but remained nearby, perhaps to give moral support if any of the others needed it.

Jay arrived within minutes followed by other officers and an ambulance. The crime scene investigators were not far behind. At the age of forty-three, Jay was fifteen years older than her sister. She was tall, stocky, and strong with short hair cut in layers around her face. A well-liked and respected member of the community, Jay was intelligent, honest, kindhearted, and hardworking.

"Tell me what you found," Jay said as she strode to the man and touched his neck repeating Shelly's earlier search for a pulse.

"We think he's dead," Juliet told her sister. "Shelly touched his arm. He's very cold. We didn't see him take any breaths."

"We got close to him. I tried to find a pulse, but I didn't feel anything and his chest isn't moving at all," Shelly informed Jay. "When I felt his cold skin, I was pretty sure he must be dead."

EMTs swarmed to the fallen man to check for vital signs and Jay, Juliet, and Shelly stepped back.

"I didn't feel a pulse either," Jay said and then she instructed the other officers to keep gawkers away from the area.

One member of the emergency medical team looked over at Jay and shook her head.

Jay cursed and pulled out her phone to alert the medical examiner as the EMTs covered the body with a sheet.

When she got off the phone, Jay moved Shelly and Juliet further to the side and asked them questions. "Tell me what happened when you arrived here."

The young women took turns reporting how they found the man, and then Juliet said, "Lauren showed up in Shelly's dream last night."

Jay made quick eye contact with Shelly. "Did she? It's been a while, hasn't it? Can you tell me about the dream?"

Shelly took a deep breath and told Jay about Lauren's appearance. "Juliet and I were running on the trails."

"Like today," Juliet said.

"Lauren was waiting at the end of the trail," Shelly said. "She put her index finger to her lips and then gestured for me to walk slowly."

"What happened then?" Jay asked.

"Lauren disappeared." Shelly shrugged. "That was it. It was brief."

Jay took a look at the body covered with a sheet. "Why do you think Lauren showed up?"

"I don't know. I have no idea."

"It's like Lauren knew about the dead man and that we were going to run in this area today," Juliet said.

Shelly gave her friend a look of disbelief. "When Lauren is in my dreams, it's only because my subconscious mind is working on some details from the day that I overlooked. I didn't know anything about this man in the park when I was dreaming."

"Well," Juliet said. "Your sister probably knew about him and came to alert you to the crime."

"That's not how I think my dreams work," Shelly said.

"But it's how *I* think they work." Juliet folded her arms over her chest. "And nothing in our experiences have proven me wrong."

"Yet," Shelly said.

"Let's leave speculation to the side and focus on what can be helpful," Jay suggested in order to end the bickering. "Did your sister communicate with you in the dream?" The question was directed to Shelly.

"Just by her hand gestures. Lauren never speaks to me in dreams."

"How did you feel during and after the dream?" Jay asked.

"During the dream I felt happy to see her, then my feelings changed to apprehensive, but curious. When I woke up, I was uneasy. Kind of shaken."

"Why do you think you felt shaken?" Jay questioned. "Was the dream disturbing in some way?"

Shelly screwed up her face in thought trying to recall the details of the dream. "Lauren seemed to be warning me of something. As soon as she disappeared in the dream, I walked forward. I think I saw something in the grass, but then I woke up and the dream ended. I don't know if there was something on the grass or not."

"Did the setting of the dream seem familiar?" Jay asked.

"Not really. We were running in the woods just like we did this morning, but I don't think the dream path was the exact path we were on earlier today. It looked slightly different."

Jay nodded. "Did either of you recognize the man in the grass?"

"He looks slightly familiar to me," Shelly said.

"I'm not sure," Juliet admitted with a frown. "I didn't look closely at his face. You know, with the blood and all."

"We'll see if he has identification on him. Let's hope so," Jay said.

"Wait." Shelly's blue eyes were wide. "I think he works at the bank in the center of town. I think I've seen him in there."

Jay nodded and stepped over to one of the other officers who handed her a wallet that was taken from the man, and after speaking at length with the EMTs and the officers, she returned to her sister and Shelly.

"The man's name is Wilson Barrett. Fifty-eight-years-old. Lives in town. His wallet was in his pocket so robbery probably wasn't the motive for the attack," Jay told them. "The medical examiner is on the way and this part of the park is going to be closed off shortly. Andrew is on the way, too." Detective Andrew Walton and Juliet had been dating for several months.

"Should we stay?" Juliet asked.

"Andrew will want to take your statements, then you can head to work. Why don't we meet later today so we can discuss where things stand?"

"Come to my house for dinner," Shelly suggested. "I'll make a chicken stir-fry."

Jay thanked the young women and strode away to deal with the crime scene.

SHELLY WAS an hour late to her job where she baked in the big kitchen of the resort's diner, but she planned to stay later in the afternoon to complete her baking tasks for the day.

"It's all anyone is talking about." Melody came into the backroom carrying some dirty plates. In her sixties, short and petite with silvery white hair, she had run the resort diner for years with her husband, Henry. "That poor man. A couple of people said he walked through the park every day on his way to and from work at the bank. He wasn't robbed. So what was it? A random attack?" Worry was written all over Melody's face as she nervously patted her chest. "What do you think about it?" she asked Shelly.

"I don't know what to say." Shelly was rolling out a pie crust on the marble countertop. "I guess we have to wait for information. The man may have had cash or credit cards in his pockets. He might have been robbed even though his wallet wasn't taken.

The robber may have been satisfied with what he removed from the man's pockets and then took off not wanting to linger in the area."

"How much could the robber have taken?" Melody asked with disgust in her voice. "A few hundred dollars? That's worth killing someone for?"

Shaking his head, Henry spoke from the grill where he was frying eggs and bacon and tending the waffle machine. "Some people have no reverence for life. We've seen it time and time again."

"At least our police force is capable and clever. They've solved so many difficult cases. We have to thank our lucky stars for that." Melody headed back to the front of the diner to take care of the customers.

"You doing okay?" Henry asked Shelly. "It wasn't an easy morning for you."

"I'm okay. I've been thinking. If Juliet and I had been earlier, we might have been able to head off the attack."

"*If only* doesn't change things," Henry said. "It's very easy to look back at something and think about how it could have been different. It doesn't matter. It worked out a certain way. We can't go back in time and make the outcome different. There's no point in giving it any thought."

"I know. You're right," Shelly sighed. "I wonder when it happened. Was he killed early this morning or was that man lying out there all night?"

"It probably happened on his way to work this morning. Wilson Barrett used to stop in here for breakfast a lot. He came in bright and early. He was always the first one at the door. Must have been an early riser."

Shelly turned to look at Henry. "You knew him?"

"I can't say we knew him. We exchanged pleasantries. A little chit chat. It's always crazy busy here in the mornings. There wasn't any time to talk."

"Why did he stop coming in?"

"He moved to the other side of town." Henry plated some eggs and toast and put the dish on the serving counter under the heat lamps so the wait-staff could pick it up and deliver it.

"Did he have a family?" Shelly asked.

"I don't know. I don't remember him ever mentioning a family. Like I said, we didn't have the opportunity to talk that much."

"Do you know anything about him?"

"He worked at one of the banks in town. He lived in the north end. Seemed like a nice guy. That's all I know." Henry cracked a few eggs over the grill.

Shelly said, "Funny, isn't it? You can pass by the

same people during the day having little interactions with them ... at the bank, the gas station, the market ... but you never really know anything about them at all."

"It's true." Henry mixed more batter for pancakes. "I wonder if the guy was in some kind of trouble."

"What sort of trouble?" Shelly carefully placed the top crust over the fruit pie and crimped the edges.

"Drugs? Gambling? Did he owe the wrong person money? Did he steal from someone? Was he involved with a married woman?" Henry speculated. "There are any number of possible scenarios that could have gotten him killed."

Shelly looked up and sighed at how naïve she was. "I didn't think of any of that. I imagined him as an innocent guy who had the misfortune to cross paths with a killer."

"That's a very real possibility, too."

"The police will figure it out," Shelly said hopefully.

"They'd better figure it out." Henry glanced over to her. "Someone killed Wilson Barrett for revenge or for kicks. Neither option is good news. We all need to stay on our toes and keep safe."

A wave of worry passed over Shelly's skin like a cold, driving rain.

3

Shelly had texted her boyfriend, Jack Graham, as soon as she left the park that morning to tell him about the body she and Juliet found. Just before she was finished with work for the day, Jack came into the diner to meet her.

"I'll drive you home," he'd said after giving her a hug and a kiss.

Shelly protested that she had her bike outside, but Jack told her he had his rack on the car so after attaching the bike to it, they headed out of the resort parking lot towards town. Ever since the accident, Shelly strongly disliked riding in any vehicles and tried to avoid it whenever possible. Jack knew how she felt and did whatever he could to support her.

"You really didn't have to drive me," Shelly told her boyfriend.

"After the morning you had, I thought you might be feeling tired." Jack moved the car onto Main Street. "I also didn't want you riding home alone with a killer on the loose."

"You're very thoughtful. I appreciate it." Shelly gave him a warm smile, and then filled him in on the details of her and Juliet's discovery. "Have you heard the victim's name? It's Wilson Barrett. He worked at the bank in the center of town. Henry was acquainted with the man and told me Mr. Barrett walked to work and back home again each day."

"He must have been walking to work when he was attacked," Jack guessed as he turned down Shelly's lane and came to a stop in front of her bungalow.

"Jay and Juliet are coming over this evening to discuss the case."

"Good. Maybe you can be of help as they move forward with the investigation," Jack said with an encouraging tone.

Jack knew that Shelly had strong perceptive skills and a unique perspective that helped her pick up on things that others overlooked, and that she was brought in to consult with Jay when cases were proving difficult.

"Maybe," Shelly said leaning in for a kiss. She really hoped the police would solve the case quickly so she wouldn't be called in to assist.

The couple made plans to meet for a bike ride the next day after work. Shelly got out and waved as Jack drove back to the resort to finish his shift.

Justice waited inside in the small entryway and when Shelly entered the house, the cat purred and purred and rubbed against the young woman's legs.

"Such a nice greeting." Shelly picked up the Calico and petted her. "It's been a crazy day. I'm glad to be home."

After showering and changing into fresh clothes, Shelly went to the kitchen to prepare the evening meal with Justice sitting in one of the kitchen chairs watching and listening to her owner talk about finding the dead man.

"Can you imagine someone attacking the man in the park?" Shelly asked the cat. "Lots of people use that park at all times of the day and evening. It was reckless to attack someone in a busy place like that. Let's hope someone saw the killer and can give a good description to the police."

Justice meowed.

"It makes you wonder about people, doesn't it? How can someone do that to another human being?" Shelly sighed as she cut up the chicken breast and placed the pieces in a bowl to marinate. "It can be a harsh world. I don't know how Jay and the other law enforcement officers can handle dealing with the worst of people day in and day out. It would really drag me down. I'm not cut out for such work."

The cat sat quietly taking in every word.

Shelly made a salad and some rice, and when Juliet and Jay arrived they sat at the kitchen table sipping wine while Shelly cooked the meal in the wok.

Jay's eyelids drooped a little from fatigue and her usual straight posture was more rounded and slouched. She leaned back in her chair with her wine glass in her hand. "The food smells delicious. I haven't eaten since breakfast."

Juliet scolded her sister. "You'll be good for nothing if you let yourself get rundown."

Shelly lit the candles on the small dining room table and the women sat down to enjoy the warm, tasty meal.

"Henry and Melody are familiar with Wilson Barrett," Shelly said. "He often went to the diner for breakfast when he lived near the resort. Henry said he didn't see the man after he moved to the other side of town."

Jay scooped the chicken and vegetables from the serving dish to her plate. "It seems Mr. Barrett walked to work each morning and walked home in the evening through the park. It was his usual routine."

"If that's the case, then someone would have known the approximate times when Barrett would be walking in the park," Juliet said.

"So was it random or was it planned?" Shelly questioned.

"That hasn't been determined yet." Jay added a spoonful of rice to her plate.

"Were there any witnesses to the crime?" Shelly passed the salad to Juliet.

"Not yet. It seems the man was probably attacked on his way home. It rained heavily in the evening which kept most people away from the park, hence no one discovered the body until you two came along early this morning."

"What do you know about Mr. Barrett?" Juliet asked.

"Barrett was fifty-eight. He'd worked at the bank for almost thirty years, although not all of that time was here in town. He started his career in the surrounding towns and his last assignment was in Paxton Park after he received a promotion."

"When was that?" Shelly asked.

"He'd been working in town for about ten years," Jay said. "Barrett was well-thought of. His colleagues liked him. His superiors gave him glowing reviews."

"Married?" Juliet asked.

"Divorced. He and his wife split up about twenty years ago. No children."

"Was it an amicable parting of the ways?" Shelly poured a bit of the homemade dressing onto her salad.

"We're looking into that," Jay said. "The ex-wife lives one town over, but has a business here in Paxton Park."

"Do you know anything about Barrett's hobbies or interests?"

"He enjoyed traveling. He played the piano. From what we've heard so far, the man was friendly and pleasant, he didn't take risks, he was kind and helpful to everyone we've spoken with. His colleagues seem truly shocked by his death. Many of them said Barrett was the last person they would have thought such a thing would happen to."

"Well, it seems someone disagreed with Barrett's colleagues," Juliet said with a raised eyebrow.

When Jay rested her fork on her plate, Shelly noticed the serious look on her face. "The attack took place right under one of the lamplights in the park. The lampposts are set along the walkways at regular intervals. The attacker chose to make his move directly under the light."

Shelly narrowed her eyes. "Do you think the attacker planned to do that? Why not hit the person when he was in a dark part of the walkway? Do you think the killer intentionally attacked Barrett in the light?"

"Right now, it seems so," Jay said.

Shelly sat up straight. "It's a bold move. Is the attacker thumbing his nose at law enforcement?"

"Or maybe at Wilson Barrett?" Juliet asked. "Was it a move to demonstrate the killer's power and aggression? Was the killer telling everyone including Mr. Barrett that he didn't need to hide in the dark? He's so good, he can kill a man in a popular park without anyone seeing him?"

Jay shook her head slowly. "It is definitely a bold move to attack someone under a lamplight. What the message is, if any, is unknown at this time."

"But you think the killer was sending a message?" Shelly asked.

"That's the way I'm leaning," Jay said. "I may be wrong. It may have just been a convenient spot. We'll see how things progress."

"Was Barrett into anything that might have led to the attack?" Juliet asked.

"We're still investigating that possibility." Jay sipped from her glass and praised Shelly for the delicious meal. "Wilson Barrett had a canister of pepper spray in his pocket. He didn't get a chance to use it."

"Even if he'd had a gun in his pocket, he prob-ably wouldn't have been able to use it since he was hit in the back of the head," Shelly said. "He *was* killed by a blow to the head, correct?"

"Yes, he was. Several blows to the head in fact, and you're right," Jay said. "Being attacked from behind would take someone by surprise and it would be very hard to react in time to save yourself. Mr. Barrett was a tall man, a bit stocky, in decent shape. If he had a warning, he might have been able to fight the attacker. The blow from behind probably incapacitated Barrett preventing him from trying to defend himself."

"Did he always carry pepper spray or was that a new thing?" Shelly's mind was working.

Jay said, "I can see we're thinking along the same lines. If Barrett recently started carrying pepper spray, he may have been worried about something. We're talking to his associates about that. So far, no one has an answer."

"Has the murder weapon been found?" Juliet asked.

"A baseball bat was found nearby, but we don't know yet if it was used in the crime," Jay reported. "As I said, it rained during the night so any blood on the bat may have been washed away. It's being tested."

"There are a lot of questions still," Shelly sighed.

"And so far, very few answers. I don't know why, but I have the feeling this is going to be a very involved and convoluted case." Jay looked to Shelly. "Let me know if your sister shows up in any more of your dreams."

Shelly nodded, but hoped Lauren wouldn't pay her any more nightly visits. For some reason, this was a crime she didn't want to get involved with.

4

The late afternoon was sunny and warm when Shelly and Jack finished their bike ride on the mountain trails and swung into town to get ice cream cones.

"Do you want to avoid the park?" Jack asked taking a lick of his chocolate chip ice cream. Whenever he and Shelly stopped in town for cones, they often took a walk through the park past the baseball diamond and around the pond.

"No, I think I'd like to take our usual walk. It's nice out. We can stay away from the crime scene."

After locking their bikes in the rack by the ice cream shop, Shelly and Jack walked hand-in-hand over to the park. The place bustled with walkers, families with little kids, a ball game going on, a couple of people having a picnic, and joggers and bicyclists moving over the walkways and paths.

"Look," Shelly said, "officers are questioning people as they pass by."

"It's a good idea," Jack nodded while he watched the police officers stop and talk to several passersby. "A lot of the same people use the park at the same time each day. Maybe one of them will recall seeing something that will help solve the crime."

Approaching the officers, Shelly and Jack spotted Juliet's boyfriend, Detective Andrew Walton with the group doing the questioning.

Andrew gave them a slight smile and a greeting when he noticed the young couple. "Out for a stroll?"

"We rode bikes and then came into town for a walk." Shelly told the detective as she licked a few drops of ice cream from her cone. "Are you having any luck?"

Thirty-year-old Andrew had dark blond hair and was tall and slim. He'd rubbed Shelly the wrong way the first time he met her when he questioned her about a crime that occurred in town not long after she'd moved to Paxton Park. She got to know him better last winter and discovered that underneath the tough-guy exterior he put on, the man was kind, honest, and funny. Juliet got to know Andrew at the same time, and she and he clicked and had been seeing each other for several months.

"Not really," Andrew told them with a frown. "It's like the park was empty when Wilson Barrett walked through on his way home last night or everyone who *was* here in the evening didn't notice anything amiss. A lot of the people we've talked to claim they didn't see one unusual thing."

"Or they're too afraid to admit seeing anything," Jack said.

"Some people don't like to get involved with cases like this," Shelly pointed out. "They're nervous about it, wary to talk. And living in a busy town with lots of tourists and townspeople around, people often don't make eye contact and just hurry along to wherever they're going without noticing what's going on around them."

"It sure seems to be the case." Andrew shrugged. "Somebody *had* to see something."

"It could have been momentarily empty in here when the attacker made his move," Jack suggested.

"Do you think the killer waited for Barrett to walk past or did he follow him into the park?" Shelly wondered out loud.

Andrew knew that Shelly helped the police with

some aspects of their cases, but he had never been told exactly in what ways she was valuable, and since he never got much of an answer when he asked about it, he'd given up trying to find out how she contributed. "Some of the stores and shops in the area have security cameras mounted outside. Officers are speaking with the owners, managers, and workers to get access to any tapes that might be available. So far, any tapes are so grainy nothing can be seen and a couple of other cameras don't even work. Some of the owners put up dummy cameras with the hope it will keep people from causing trouble." Andrew shook his head. "Studies show that functional cameras don't really deter bad behavior, but they can be useful in cases like this if there are tapes to review."

"Jay told me a baseball bat was found under the trees near the body," Shelly said.

"There's nothing conclusive yet, but there's some chatter that the bat is not the murder weapon," Andrew said. "Some divers went into the lake today to search for a possible weapon that might have been tossed into the water. Nothing was found. We're coming up empty all around."

"Too bad." A forlorn look clouded Shelly's face.

Andrew shoved his hands into his pockets. "I

don't know how someone can get killed in a heavily-used park without anyone noticing a single thing."

"Well," Jack said, "it *was* nearly dark at the time."

"It's very well-lit here," Andrew pointed out. "And the person attacked Barrett under the lights."

"What are your thoughts on that?" Shelly asked the detective.

Andrew looked at the young woman. "How do you mean?"

"Do you think the killer deliberately attacked Barrett in the light? Wouldn't it have been smarter to make his move when Barrett walked into an area of darkness?"

"It would have been a heck of a lot smarter," Andrew agreed. "But he struck under the light, and so far it hasn't led to him being caught."

"Do you think the attacker was deliberately acting in a bold way?" Jack asked. He and Shelly had been discussing why someone would attack a victim under the bright lamplight.

Before answering Jack, Andrew watched one of the officers approach an older couple to ask them questions. "It's a possibility. It's also possible that Barrett realized he was under attack and began to run. The killer wanted him silenced as quickly as possible so he just happened to hit Barrett under the light."

Something about what Andrew said bothered Shelly. "But if Barrett knew the killer was after him, wouldn't he have pulled out his pepper spray? Or at the very least, fumbled for it? Maybe dropped it as he tried to run away? It wouldn't still be in his pocket, would it?"

"That depends," Andrew said. "If Barrett noticed the killer coming at him, his first instinct was probably to flee. He may not have wasted any time fiddling around for his pepper spray."

"I guess not."

"I'd better get back to speaking with passersby," Andrew said. "Juliet told me the four of us are meeting for dinner this weekend. It will be good for me to get out with friends and relax. I'm looking forward to it."

Shelly and Jack agreed and said goodbye to the detective and then continued their walk around the park.

"They're really working hard on this case," Jack said. "It was bad luck that it rained the night Barrett was killed. Evidence was probably lost or ruined."

The sun had nearly set and the park was falling into darkness.

"Would you mind walking past the crime scene?" Shelly asked. "I'd like to go past the area to see how it looked in the dark."

"Sure." Jack looked slightly surprised by the suggestion, but he was more than willing to go along.

"From what Henry told me at the diner, Mr. Barrett walked home from the bank just about every night," Shelly explained. "The bank is back that way." She looked to the south. "Barrett's house is on the north side of town. He must have entered the park the same way we did, then followed this path up the hill to cut over to the other side. It would be shorter than walking around to his house by way of the streets."

"It's nicer in the park, too," Jack added. "After being cooped up inside all day, Barrett probably enjoyed walking in nature, seeing kids playing, hearing the birds, passing by the trees and the wide expanses of grass. It must have been a good way to unwind after the work day."

After walking a little further, Shelly stopped and pointed to the cordoned off section of the walkway. Two officers stood nearby to make sure no one disturbed the scene.

"That's where we saw him. We came out of the

woods on the trail over there." Shelly pointed to the opening between the trees. "I wasn't sure what was on the grass. I think at first, the mind doesn't want to entertain the idea that what it's seeing might be a dead body so it runs through every other possibility before returning to the worst outcome."

"You're probably right." Jack nodded. "When I was in combat, it was necessary to force the mind to expect the worst. Otherwise, you might not get another chance to react in a way that protected yourself and your buddies."

Shelly turned to look into her boyfriend's eyes. "I sometimes forget how hard it must have been for you when you were in the military. Is it better if we stop talking about death and crime and criminals?"

"It's okay." Jack put his arm around Shelly. "There are lots of things I'd like to forget about being in the service, but now that you're in my life, those memories are softening and they don't get to me like they used to."

"I'm glad. Why don't we head back to get the bikes and go to my place? We can make popcorn and watch a movie." Shelly smiled. "And besides, I think Justice would like to cuddle up with you."

Jack laughed. "I could never disappoint a cat, especially not Justice."

As they started back the way they'd come, Shelly took a quick look back to where Wilson Barrett had fallen on the grass and died. The spot was fully illuminated by the streetlamp and the ground glowed in the golden light.

A strange spot to kill someone.

5

Shelly and Jay walked into the swanky accounting office that belonged to Tina Barrett, the murder victim's ex-wife. Floor to ceiling windows looked out over the town and at the majestic mountains rising in the distance. It was late afternoon and Shelly had completed her workday baking the pastries for the diner and the bakery-café located in the resort's promenade of stores and shops.

Tina Barrett's heels could be heard tapping on the wood floor before she came around the corner to the reception area. Shelly and Jay turned and introduced themselves to the woman. Wearing a black skirt and navy blazer, fifty-eight-year-old Tina was of medium-height, slender, and had chin-length auburn hair.

With a warm, welcoming smile, she shook hands with the visitors, who offered their condolences.

"I can't believe what happened. Wilson murdered? It's mind-boggling." Tina led them to her office at the end of the hallway where she invited them to take seats on the modern gray sofas. The room was stylishly decorated in soft grays and blues.

Bottles of water sat next to glasses on a wooden tray in the center of the coffee table and Tina offered tea and coffee.

Jay began by thanking her for seeing them. "You have a beautiful office."

"We've been here for five years. I felt it was important to have a comfortable space. We have a number of high-end clients who have second or third homes here in town and in the surrounding area who expect a certain atmosphere." Tina smiled. "We want to keep them as clients."

"How many accountants do you have working with you?" Jay asked.

"There are five of us as well as the support staff. We don't want to get any bigger. We're happy with the way things are."

"You and Wilson had been married for a number

of years before parting ways?" Jay began her questioning.

Tina was business-like in describing their marriage and divorce. "We were married for about thirteen years. We grew apart. Our divorce was amicable. We felt it was the best thing for both of us. There were no kids to consider. We split our assets and that was it."

"Did you and Wilson stay in touch?" Jay questioned.

"We did. We'd talk on the phone, occasionally meet for coffee, though not that often, would run into each other at charity or business events." Tina opened a bottle of water and poured it into a cut-glass goblet.

"When was the last time you saw Wilson?"

Tina took a swallow from the glass. "Let's see. A month ago? I stopped into the bank."

"How was Wilson when you saw him? Did you notice anything different about his mood?" Jay asked.

Tina paused to think about the question. "No, I don't recall anything in particular. He seemed busy, but he was pleasant. We didn't talk at length. He had a meeting."

"Had Wilson confided anything that was bothering him? Anything he was worried about?"

Tina shook her head slowly. "No. Nothing. I probably wouldn't be the person Wilson would confide in. We were cordial, but we weren't really friends."

Shelly was slightly surprised that the woman had yet to show any sadness or deep concern that her ex-husband had been murdered. She knew they'd been divorced for twenty years, but she expected a little more emotion from a person who had once shared her life with Wilson. "Who would he have confided in?"

Tina blinked at Shelly like she'd almost forgotten she was sitting with them ... the young woman had been so quiet to that point.

"Um. Well, he was dating a woman. Her name is Imelda Wallace. They've been casually dating for a couple of years. Wilson had two close friends, Bill Handy and Mike Meeks. Maybe they'd know if something was bothering Wilson."

Jay asked, "What was Wilson like?"

"He was a good person, smart, easy-going. He had a kind way about him. Wilson was serious about his career, but I'd say he wasn't that ambitious. I thought he could do more, aim a little higher, but he was often content with things as they were. He didn't push himself to be more successful." Tina sat straighter. "Of course, there's nothing wrong with that, but I'm more high-energy, more ambitious and driven. He wanted a more low-key life. Our different natures and what we wanted from life could sometimes conflict."

"Did Wilson like his job?"

"I believe he did. I don't think he cared to rise any further at the bank. He seemed happy with where he was. I think he would have liked to retire in a few years."

"Did he have any hobbies?"

"He played piano. He loved music. He enjoyed traveling."

"What about family members?" Jay asked despite having heard that Wilson's father was alive and living two towns over. You never knew if there was some black-sheep family member no one ever talked about.

"Wilson was an only child," Tina said. "His mother died when he was a teenager. His father is in a nursing home. At least, I think he is. He must be in his nineties. I never heard he passed away."

"Was Wilson close to his father?" Shelly asked.

"He was, though the man has had dementia for

years now. I know Wilson visited him, but I don't know how regularly."

Jay asked the next question. "Do you have any inklings about who might have attacked Wilson?"

Tina's eyes went wide and she leaned back. "Me? I have no idea. I thought it was a random attack. Wasn't it?"

"We're trying to determine the circumstances of the incident," Jay told the woman.

"You think Wilson knew his attacker?" Tina's voice had risen an octave.

Jay carefully phrased her reply. "It is presently unknown if Wilson knew the person who made the attack on him."

"Well. I assumed it was a robbery gone bad." Tina nervously tucked a strand of hair behind her ear. "Was Wilson robbed?"

"There are some details we're unable to divulge to the public as it's an active investigation."

"Oh. Well. I see." Tina reached for her water glass and took another long sip before looking from Shelly to Jay. "Was Wilson involved in something dangerous? Something illegal?"

"Why would you ask that?" Jay questioned, keeping her voice even.

Tina shook her head as if she were trying to

organize her thoughts. "He was walking through a central park in town. It wasn't late. People were around. The park is used by lots of people. Wilson walks through that park every day. If it wasn't a random robbery, which is unbelievable in itself, who would attack him? What would be the reason?" The woman's eyes darkened. "Did it look like a professional job?"

Jay deflected the question. "What sort of questionable thing could Wilson have been involved in?"

Tina's cheeks flushed slightly. "I wouldn't know. How would I know?"

"You saw him on occasion," Jay said. "He might have spoken to you about something he was uncomfortable talking about with close friends. He may have needed some advice, so he reached out for your input. We aren't suggesting you were mixed up in anything, only that Wilson may have come to you for guidance."

"No." Tina's face tightened. "No. I have no idea. Wilson didn't ask me for advice. He didn't tell me anything about questionable activities." The woman pressed her hand against her cheek. "Gosh. What could Wilson have gotten himself mixed up in?"

"Most likely, nothing at all," Jay said calmly. "We have to consider every option in cases like these. It's a basic part of the investigatory process. Random attacks happen. There are often no good rational reasons as to why they occur."

"Well, I didn't speak with Wilson about anything that wasn't aboveboard. I never heard he was doing anything shady. He may have been, but I wasn't involved in any way."

A knock came on the door and Tina's assistant popped her head in. "Your client is here."

"Thank you," Tina told the assistant and then looked at her visitors. "I'm sorry. I have a meeting now."

Shelly and Jay thanked the accountant for her time and left the office.

Once outside on the sidewalk, Jay asked, "What did you think?"

Shelly said, "I think Tina wanted us to have no reason to believe she was mixed up in anything Wilson might have been doing. She may have been a little too energetic in her denials."

"Hmm. My thoughts exactly." As they walked to the small parking lot behind the office building, Jay checked her phone for messages from the other investigators. "The woman may only be shaken up at the thought Wilson got himself killed by getting involved in something illegal and may know nothing at all about what was going on."

"On the other hand, maybe she did know something and wants to keep that fact hidden from law enforcement," Shelly suggested. "You'll keep the possibility in mind?"

"I sure will. How would you like to pay a visit to Imelda Wallace, Wilson's girlfriend?" Jay asked. "She may have been someone Wilson would have confided in."

Shelly agreed to go along with Jay when she interviewed the girlfriend. "From what you know so far about Wilson Barrett, would you expect he could have been involved in something illegal?"

Jay unlocked the doors of the vehicle and before getting in, she looked at Shelly over the roof of the car.

"I could be wrong, but Wilson Barrett doesn't strike me as someone who would voluntarily enter into trouble."

"That's the impression I'm getting, too," Shelly said. "I'm also wondering if someone may have forced him to do something he wouldn't have done on his own."

Jay nodded. "It's something to think about."

Shelly said, "There are a number of possibilities.

It was a random attack. Wilson did nothing wrong, but someone held a grudge against the man that festered into a criminal act. Or Wilson got involved with the wrong people over something and one of those people decided to take his life."

"That about covers it," Jay said. "All we can do is follow those strands and see where they take us."

Shelly got into the car, full of worry about where the strands might lead them.

6

Mr. Barrett's girlfriend, Imelda Wallace, was fifty-years-old, had shoulder-length, wavy, brown hair and dark brown eyes, and an athletic build. When she opened the door to Jay and Shelly, the rims of the woman's eyes were red and she was clutching a tissue in one of her hands.

"Please come in." Imelda led them into her small, pretty, well-tended cottage located in a neighborhood of similar homes tucked into the base of the mountain about two miles from the center of town. The living room was decorated with a Scandinavian flavor, no clutter, soft colors, green plants, a modern sofa, and two comfortable side chairs set in front of a stone fireplace. A small brown dog sat at attention on the multi-colored rug with his eyes glued on its owner.

"This is Buddy. He's the best dog. He stays with me all the time. Ever since Wilson died, Buddy's been quiet and less active. I think he's picking up on my sorrow."

Shelly bent down and the dog hurried over to her, eager to meet the new person, and after some patting, Shelly took a seat by the fireplace.

"Do you have some news about Wilson?" Imelda looked hopefully at Jay.

"I'm afraid not." Jay took a small notebook and pen from her jacket pocket. "The visit is simply a follow-up to our previous conversation. For Shelly's benefit, would you mind giving some information about your background and your relationship with Wilson?"

Imelda did not seem bothered by having to run through another description of her time with Wilson. She took in a deep breath and began her summary. "I've lived in Paxton Park since I was a teenager. My family moved here from Maine. I own a boutique on a street that runs off of Main. I've had it for about ten years. Before that I was a merchandiser at the resort."

54

"And when did you meet Wilson Barrett?" Jay asked.

Imelda made a little sniffing sound, but she held her emotions in check. "I met Wilson about two years ago. He came into my shop for a new necktie. We chatted." A smile spread over the woman's face. "We hit it off immediately. We flirted a little. Wilson was going to leave the store after purchasing the tie and I was afraid I wouldn't run into him again so I asked him out for coffee. I've never done such a thing before, but I felt like we had a nice connection. I liked Wilson right away. I felt comfortable with him. He was a very kind man." Imelda's words caught in her throat and she had to pause to collect herself. "I'm sorry."

"If you'd like to get some water or take a break, we wouldn't mind at all," Jay said.

"I'm okay." Imelda pushed her shoulders back. "I want to help. I want to help you catch the person who took Wilson's life."

"You and Wilson kept your own places?" Shelly asked.

"We did. I know it's unusual, but we both liked having our own homes. We spent plenty of time at each other's places. We liked it that way since we both enjoyed time on our own. It seemed to keep the magic in our relationship. It always seemed like we were out on a date when we were together." Imelda shrugged. "It worked for us."

"You and Wilson were together for two years? Was marriage ever discussed?" Jay asked.

"It was discussed, but always tabled. We felt like we were married to each other already. There was really no need to formalize what we had. I have two children from a previous marriage. Wilson and I weren't going to have kids together. We didn't see the need to have a ceremony to tie the knot ... we'd already tied our hearts together." A tear ran down the woman's cheek and she dabbed at it with the tissue.

Buddy, the dog, hurried over and lay down at the woman's feet.

Shelly's throat tightened with sadness at what Imelda had lost with Wilson.

Jay coughed and asked, "When did you see Wilson last?"

"The night before he was attacked. He had dinner here. We watched a movie. He stayed over and went to work in the morning."

"Did Wilson seem himself?" Shelly asked.

"Yes, he did. We had a very pleasant evening together." Imelda's lower lip began to tremble.

Shelly followed up. "Had he mentioned being worried about anything?"

"Not really. His work could be demanding. The home office was always wanting to implement some new thing. Wilson had to keep up with new regulations and laws. He had to keep the employees happy. There was always some customer fussing about something or other."

Jay's interest was piqued by Imelda's statement. "Was Wilson dealing with a customer who may have been more disgruntled than usual?"

"I wouldn't say that. I don't think so."

"Did Wilson feel safe at work?" Jay asked.

Imelda's eyebrows went up. "Well, we often hear about a gunman entering a public space and shooting people. A school, a concert, a restaurant, a financial institution. We talked about working with the public, about the potential for trouble, but it was just idle chatter. Neither of us felt any real danger at our jobs."

"Did Wilson ever worry about a certain employee or a particular customer?"

"Not seriously, not as if a person might do something dangerous. Sometimes people were bothersome, but not so much that Wilson thought he might be in danger."

"What about you?" Shelly asked. "Did you ever have difficulty with a customer or an acquaintance?"

Imelda shook her head. "Nothing that would lead to Wilson losing his life over."

"We heard that Wilson's father is in a nursing home?"

"That's right. Over in Rollingwood. It took Wilson quite a while to find the right place. You know how some nursing homes aren't the best. He wanted his father to be comfortable and well-taken care of."

"How is the father doing?"

Imelda gave a little shrug. "He's not great. He has dementia. Many times, he didn't even recognize his son. That was hard on Wilson, even though he understood."

"Has the father been told what happened to Wilson?" Jay questioned.

"No one told him," Imelda said. "What's the point? It might upset him initially, but then he wouldn't remember what he'd been told. Why cause the man any heartache, even if it was brief? I'll keep visiting him. He has no one else now that his son is gone."

"What about friends? Did Wilson have some close friends?"

"He had two good friends. Mike Meeks is a lawyer over in Newell and Bill Handy teaches shop at the high school. They liked to get together to watch sports or a movie. They went out for dinner together, met up regularly to play cards. They were all musicians and liked to play together."

"Were they in a band together?"

"Oh, no. They played just for fun."

"Had they been friends for a long time?" Shelly asked.

"Decades. Wilson met Mike skiing on the mountain a long time ago and became friends with Bill when they played on a softball team together."

"So Wilson skied," Jay said. "Did he have any other hobbies?"

"He liked walking the trails. Wilson loved to be out in nature. He loved this town, loved being so close to the mountains."

The more Shelly learned about Wilson Barrett, the more she liked him. She appreciated the man's desire for a balanced life, his love of the outdoors, the kind way he seemed to treat the people in his life. Why would someone want him dead? Was it a random attack? If it was, how would the police ever gather enough clues to identify the perpetrator? Was someone going to get away with murder?

"Was there anyone who didn't like Wilson?" Jay's question pulled Shelly out of her thoughts.

Imelda stared at the police officer. "I don't ... think so."

Jay rephrased what she'd asked. "Was there anyone who was angry with Wilson?"

Imelda swallowed. "Not that I know of."

"Had Wilson been distracted lately?"

Shelly wondered if Jay's sudden rapid fire questions were meant to rattle Imelda so she would slip up about something she might be trying to conceal.

"Work was busy for him. He had things on his mind, but I wouldn't say he was distracted." Imelda's dog jumped into her lap and she hugged him.

"Had he been working later than usual?"

"Sometimes he did."

"Lately?" Jay asked.

Imelda nodded. "The past couple of weeks."

"Did Wilson always carry pepper spray with him?" Jay questioned.

"Pepper spray?" Imelda's forehead scrunched up in confusion. "Wilson didn't have any pepper spray."

Shelly exchanged a quick look with Jay.

Jay said in gentle tone of voice, "Wilson had pepper spray in his pocket when he was found in the park."

Imelda blinked at the two people in her living room. "He did? He never had any pepper spray. I never once saw him with any. Why would he have that?"

Jay again asked the questions she'd asked earlier in the interview. "Was Wilson worried about anything? Was he afraid of someone?"

Imelda's eyes filled with tears.

Buddy stood up on her lap and gave the woman a soft lick on the wrist.

Imelda's hand shook when she reached over to pat her dog. "I ... I just don't know."

7

Shelly finished the last of the pies and set them on the counter to cool. Once or twice a week, she baked in the commercial kitchen of the Glad Hill Farm and Orchard to supplement the pies, cakes, and cookies made by their full-time baker. In the fall, Shelly upped her hours at the farm to meet the demand for fruit pies.

Glad Hill Farm was only a mile away from the edge of town and was popular with both tourists and townsfolk for its many attractions. A brewery, petting zoo, general store, and lake were at one end of the acreage while the orchard was located only about a quarter mile away. Pathways linked the different parts of the farm and visitors strolled from one end to the other. A huge corn maze drew massive crowds in the autumn.

The food barn was set up like a general store where products were sold from the farm, while the rest of the building served lunch, snacks, drinks, and ice cream. The interior had beautiful, rich wood walls, soaring ceilings, tables and chairs, and crystal chandeliers hanging from the rafters. Huge windows on one side brought in the sunlight and the barn doors on the opposite side could be opened to provide a gorgeous view of the landscape.

Shelly decided to look for the owner, Dwayne Thomas, so she stepped outside to follow the path over to the lake where the man often enjoyed sitting in the sun on a bench overlooking the water. Not long ago, a relative of Dwayne's had been slowly poisoning the older man in a scheme to get rid of him in order to take over the farm. Shelly had discovered the evil plan in time to save Dwayne's life and the two had become good friends.

When Shelly spotted him sitting on his usual bench, she waved and he gave her a wide smile as he scooted to the side to make room for her.

In his seventies, Dwayne had a thin, wiry build and a head of white hair. He'd spent his life doing manual labor at his farm and had the shoulder and arm muscles to show for it. He and Shelly shared another connection ... Dwayne had lost his wife and son to an automobile accident over fifteen years ago and he and the young woman had talked together for hours about loss, grief, and carrying on with life even though part of your heart was missing.

"I was hoping to see you today," Dwayne patted the seat bench for Shelly to sit. "If you didn't come along in a few minutes, I was going to hunt you down in the kitchen."

"I always look for you." Shelly chuckled. "You know I wouldn't leave without talking with you."

"How did the baking go?"

"Very well. I had to get out of the kitchen though. The pies smelled so great, I would have eaten all of them if I didn't leave."

With a smile, Dwayne adjusted his baseball hat to better shade his eyes. "It's a beautiful day. I love this time of year, everything green and lush, so much promise in the air."

"Me, too. Winter can be fun and beautiful here, but it's the warm weather I love the most," Shelly agreed.

"What's the news about Wilson Barrett? You talk to Jay about what's going on?" Dwayne asked.

"A lot of dead ends. They're knee-deep in the investigation."

"Any motive?"

"Not yet," Shelly sighed.

"Heck of a thing. Attacked while walking in the park. That park is almost like a town common so many people use it. It was near dark, of course, but it wasn't late at night. It was kind of a reckless thing to do with people around. It's not a remote or quiet location."

"That's what a lot of people think. The only thing is, the killer has gotten away with it. So far, at least."

"Do you know where in the park the attack took place?" Dwayne asked.

Shelly shifted on the bench to face the man. "Juliet and I were out running the trails that morning. We're the ones who found Mr. Barrett."

Dwayne sucked in a breath of air and made a whooshing sound of disbelief. "You? And Juliet? You know, if folks didn't know you two, they'd begin to get suspicious of you both. You've previously found two victims of a killer. Am I right?"

"Just one, before Mr. Barrett."

"There was the young woman in the woods and there was Grant Norris in the barn at the resort."

"Oh. Right."

"You see what I mean?" Dwayne asked. "People might wonder why you and Juliet are always stumbling onto crime scenes."

Shelly frowned. "People should be wondering why on earth there are so many crimes committed around here."

Dwayne shrugged. "Even though we're out in the woods, as far as crime goes, it's more like a big city. Lots of people coming and going. Tourists around all year long, and lots of them put their guard down because they're on vacation. On top of that, it's easy for bad people to get lost in the crowd. Heavily populated or visited areas are magnets for a subset of criminals."

"Huh," Shelly grunted. "Maybe I should move back to Boston."

"What do you think?" Dwayne asked. "Was it a random attack on Wilson?"

"I just don't know. Nothing is pointing one way or another, but Jay and the other officers will figure it out."

Dwayne nodded. "We're lucky to have such a competent law enforcement department here in town."

A gentle breeze kicked up off the lake and sent a whisper of cool air in Shelly and Dwayne's direction.

Looking over the lake and to the forest and mountains rising in the distance, Shelly knew she would never want to leave Paxton Park. Wilson Barrett's girlfriend hinted at the man's love for the town and talked about how he'd lived in the area most of his life. The thought caused Shelly's heart to sink.

Who crossed paths with him? Why the urge to murder the man? Was the killer out for revenge or was the attacker in a murderous mindset and happened upon Barrett by chance?

"I knew him slightly," Dwayne said taking Shelly out of her thoughts.

"Did you?"

"I did business at the bank he worked at."

"I have an account there, too, but I only knew who Mr. Barrett was from seeing him in his office," Shelly said. "I don't think we ever interacted."

"*We* did. He'd helped me with a few loans I took out to expand the farm with the brewery and the addition of the food barn. Wilson was a nice person. He played piano. Until recently, he played in that fancy restaurant at the resort several evenings a week. My sister dragged me there a few times. So expensive. It's ridiculous to spend so much money on a meal." Dwayne shook his head.

"A lot of people enjoy fine dining." Shelly smiled.

"I didn't know Wilson played piano there. Why did he stop?"

"He told me it was taking up too much of his time. He'd done it for a long time." Dwayne removed his hat, wiped at his brow, and replaced the cap. "Wilson taught an evening class in basic financial stuff like keeping a budget, renting or buying a home, how to build your savings, the basics of investing."

"Where? At the college?"

"No, at the high school. Those adult enrichment courses. He didn't think people knew enough about their finances and that could lead some folks into crushing debt. Working at the bank, Wilson saw a lot of people who were in financial trouble. He wanted to do what he could to help people avoid money problems."

Shelly looked at Dwayne and asked, "Did Wilson ever mention trouble with anyone? Either at the restaurant when he was playing or maybe, at the bank, or in the course he was teaching?"

"I don't recall him complaining about anyone in particular."

Shelly's eyes narrowed in thought. "It seems he came into contact with a lot of different people, at the bank, playing at the restaurant, teaching the course. I wonder if he crossed paths with the wrong person somewhere along the line?"

"And then that person killed him?" Dwayne looked alarmed. "For what reason?"

"Some people don't need much of a reason," Shelly said with a tone of resignation in her voice. She had seen a lot since coming to Paxton Park and was always baffled at the misery human beings could inflict on one another. "Some people misinterpret things and blow them out of proportion. They take an unintended slight and turn it into something big and react with fury to it. There are plenty of people who can't control their emotions, who are full of anger, who have the need to strike out at others."

"I know that all too well." Dwayne huffed in disgust thinking about his own relative who attempted to kill him. "There are some who are incredibly greedy and selfish and who only consider their own needs and wants ... and they don't care who they hurt to get it. Those people are lacking in empathy ... or some other basic human characteristic. Unfortunately, Wilson must have run into one of them."

Shelly gave a nod. "I guess I should head home. Can I walk with you back to the barn?"

Dwayne pushed himself off the bench. "If I give these bones of mine a rest, then they protest when I try to get them moving again."

Shelly chuckled. "Actually, I don't blame them."

Dwayne slipped his arm through Shelly's as they walked along the path back to the food barn. "Don't you and Juliet get mixed up in this mess. Steer clear of it. Leave the police to do their thing. Don't get anywhere near it. You hear me?"

"I do." Shelly patted the man's arm.

But unfortunately, it's too late to back away.

8

When Shelly and Juliet arrived for the evening community meeting organized by the Paxton Park Police department, the high school auditorium was packed with people. Television crews and reporters clustered at the sides of the stage.

Finding a seat in the back row, they settled in, eager to hear what the community leaders had to say about the murder investigation.

"I didn't expect so many people to attend." Juliet glanced around the room which was already becoming sticky and warm.

"There's a lot of concern in town," Shelly said. "The park is a popular gathering spot. People have always felt safe there. Now they feel that the place has been violated and they want answers."

A group of men and woman came onto the stage from the right side.

"There's Jay," Shelly said.

"And Andrew." Juliet smiled at her boyfriend even though he didn't see her way back in the auditorium.

The mayor, the assistant district attorney, several other officers, and the police chief filed across the stage and most of them took seats in the gray, metal chairs set in a row.

When Mayor Clay Daniels stepped up to the podium, a flurry of flashes went off as reporters took pictures. In his sixties, trim, and tall, the mayor could be abrasive and smug, and many in the community didn't care for him and were eager for someone to oust the man. "Thank you all for coming. We called the meeting to update everyone on the investigation into Wilson Barrett's death." The man droned on for several minutes about what law enforcement had done so far, what had been learned, and what was planned as they moved forward. He then introduced the police chief.

Chief Thomas Lancaster was in his late sixties, thick in the shoulders, stocky, and trim in the waist.

He still had a full head of brown hair and many speculated he dyed it to retain his youthful appearance. The chief ran through the timeline of the attack on Mr. Barrett. When he discussed how the man was found in the park, he only mentioned *two citizens discovered the body*, careful not to reveal Shelly's or Juliet's name.

The chief cleared his throat and went on. "Mr. Barrett had been hit on the head several times resulting in serious head wounds. It is assumed that the attacker approached from behind and when within striking distance, he landed the first blow. It is also assumed that Mr. Barrett was struck unaware and did not have ample warning to defend himself. It appears that the victim fell to his knees and was hit several more times. It was dark when the attack took place. Rain started around 7:30pm and continued for several hours. We put the time of the attack between six-thirty and seven in the evening. This was determined by security footage from the bank where Mr. Barrett worked. He is seen leaving the bank at 6:15pm. Barrett routinely walked home from work which would have placed him at the park at around 6:25. He was attacked as he walked up the slight hill that would take him to the neighborhood on the other side of the park."

Jay was next to speak and she gave some details about the investigation and where it was headed. "A baseball bat was recovered from under the trees near the body, but it has been determined that it is *not* the murder weapon. Divers have searched the lake, but nothing was found there. Presently, we have no suspects. We ask the public to contact the police department if they saw anything at the park that evening. Any small thing can end up being of the utmost importance. Please do not disregard anything you might have seen."

The assistant district attorney briefly took the podium and assured the crowd that everything was being done that could be done. Then all of the speakers stood near the microphone to take questions. The audience was told to make two lines and that they would all be able to ask their questions.

The first to speak was an older woman with gray hair. "Are we safe?"

The chief spoke. "You should take the precautions you always do as you go about your day. Keep your doors locked, don't walk alone late at night, don't walk alone in deserted areas, if you see something that makes you uncomfortable then go into a store or seek out places with other people around, call the police. If you take precautions, then you will keep yourselves safe."

"Why is it so hard to find the killer?" A young man demanded.

Jay took the question and did a good job of explaining the intricacies of crimes and investigations. "Sometimes, there are very few clues to go on and the investigation takes a good amount of time to make the necessary discoveries."

"I would die if I had to face these community questions," Juliet whispered to her friend. "I don't like to be on the spot and have to come up with an articulate answer on demand. Imagine having to do this with television crews recording your every word? I'd make a fool of myself and then I'd have to move away in shame."

Shelly had to bite her lip to keep from chuckling at Juliet's comment. "Then it's a good thing it's Jay up there and not you."

"Do you know anything about how the attacker looks?" A middle-aged man asked the panel. "Like from security cameras in the area?"

The police chief said, "We don't have a description as yet."

"Why did the killer attack Mr. Barrett in a lighted area? Why not wait until he moved into a dark spot?"

This question was from an older man. "Isn't that a bold move? Have there been any other similar crimes that have taken place in neighboring towns? Or anywhere in the state for that matter?"

Jay responded, "It may seem that the attacker was behaving in a bold manner because he attacked Mr. Barrett in the lighted area, however, Mr. Barrett may have detected someone too close to him and sped up, or maybe he was about to run. The attacker wouldn't want Mr. Barrett to yell or cry out or try to run away so he quickly took his opportunity ... which happened to be under the lamppost."

A young mother with two little kids with her asked the next question. "Should we keep away from the park? We go there all the time."

Mayor Daniels stepped to the podium. "You should certainly continue to enjoy the park, but .... you should avoid the place after dark. If Mr. Barrett heeded that, he would still be alive."

Boos went up from the crowd.

A man stood up from his auditorium seat and spoke with an angry tone. "Most of us go to the park in the dark. There are baseball games and basketball games going on at night under the lights. Most of the area is well-lit. It's always been a safe place. Sure, it's taking a chance to walk around in there at midnight or whatever, but Mr. Barrett was killed around 6:30pm. To paint him as being irresponsible for going through the park in the early evening when there are plenty of people around is outrageous. Barrett did nothing wrong. He did something lots of us do. And we aren't behaving in a reckless fashion by being in the park in the dark in the evening."

A number of people applauded the speaker.

Mayor Daniels got red in the face. "Tonight the police talked about taking precautions. I'm sorry if you think I'm being insensitive, but being in a park at night is not a smart thing to do. You need to understand how to take the correct precautions to ensure your safety."

People began discussing the matter with those sitting next to them, some men and women shouted their opinions at the mayor, and the meeting began to devolve into disarray.

Shelly and Juliet watched the commotion as the assistant district attorney tried to take charge and restore order.

"Mayor Daniels certainly knows how to work a crowd." Shelly rolled her eyes.

"The man doesn't know when to quit. Look at the television crews," Juliet said as TV cameras began swiveling around to film the audience. "They weren't expecting things to devolve into a shouting match."

"The man who said the mayor's comment was insensitive was right," Shelly pointed out. "Mayor Daniels shouldn't have criticized Mr. Barrett for walking in the park at dinner time whether it was dark outside or not. It wasn't late. It's always been a safe place."

"Until now," Juliet sighed. "Have you had enough? How about we head home?"

Once outside of the hot and humid auditorium, the young women appreciated the cool evening air as they strolled away from the school and turned onto Main Street.

"I hope it doesn't turn into a brawl back there," Juliet said.

"Maybe we got out just in time," Shelly kidded. "We can watch the news later to see how things ended up."

"Do you think the meeting was helpful? I mean before the shouting match started."

"I guess so," Shelly said. "I think talking about what happened and discussing what steps the police are taking in the investigation can be reassuring to people."

"It sort of made me feel more nervous. They

called a big community meeting. It almost makes the whole thing scarier, if that's even possible. A murder is already scary when the killer is still on the loose," Juliet said. "Do you think the killer is from around here?"

Shelly shrugged. "I have no idea."

"Sometimes I find myself looking over my shoulder to be sure no one is sneaking up on me," Juliet said taking a quick backwards glance. "There's no way to defend yourself if someone sneaks up on you and hits you with something on the back of the head."

Thinking about an attack from behind caused a shiver of terror to run over Shelly's skin. "Maybe we should sign up for a self-defense class," she said to her friend before taking a peek over her own shoulder.

9

Right before the knock sounded on her door, Shelly and Justice had settled on the sofa after eating an early dinner. Disturbed by the rapping noise, Justice jumped up on the back of the couch and swished her tail back and forth while staring at the front door.

Shelly looked through the peephole to see a man standing on her porch. Leaving the security chain on, she opened the door a little.

"Can I help you?" she asked.

Just under six feet tall and stocky, the man looked to be in his late sixties. His light brown hair was thinning on top. He wore tan slacks and a navy blazer.

"Shelly Taylor? I'm Mike Meeks. I was a friend of

Wilson Barrett. Imelda Wallace told me you spoke with her. Do you have a few minutes to talk?" He held out his driver's license and a business card. "Here are two things to prove who I am. Would you be able to meet me at the coffee shop around the corner? I wouldn't expect you to feel comfortable inviting a stranger into your home."

Shelly looked at the pieces of identification and handed them back to the man. "I can meet you at the coffee shop. Give me five minutes to change."

"Thanks. I'll see you in a little while." Mike Meeks nodded and returned to the BMW he had parked in front of the house.

When Shelly closed the door, she made eye contact with Justice. "That was unexpected. I wonder why he wants to speak with me? Hopefully, he has some information to share."

Justice let out a loud meow.

Mike Meeks waved to Shelly when she walked into the coffee house and she went over to his table to join him. Extending her hand to shake, she introduced herself. She ordered a cup of tea and it was delivered within a few minutes. "You and Wilson were friends?"

"For years. Decades, really. It's quite a shock to think of him gone." Mike took a swallow of coffee.

When he didn't say anything more, Shelly asked, "You spoke with Imelda?"

"She said you and a police officer went by to talk with her about Wilson. I went to the community meeting, but I was wondering if there was any more information about what happened? Maybe something the police don't want to bring up to the public? Since you're working with the police, I thought I'd ask you."

"I'm really not involved in the investigation itself," Shelly said trying to explain her association with law enforcement without mentioning her dreams. "I help the police on occasion by keeping notes at an interview, doing some research for them. I'm not an officer and they don't share the details of an investigation with me so I really don't know any more than you do."

"I see," Mike said, his face showing his disappointment. "Were you at the community meeting?"

"I was. I went as a concerned town resident though, not as an assistant to the police."

"What did you think of the meeting?"

"It was helpful in some ways." Shelly explained that she thought a meeting like that could calm some townspeople by being reassured the police were doing all they could, but that it also might cause more anxiety for other residents because there were no suspects and the investigation seemed to have stalled.

"I agree with everything you said," Mike told her. "For me, I have to admit that the lack of suspects is disturbing. It can be worrisome to townspeople to think a killer is freely walking around."

"It makes me uneasy as well." Shelly nodded.

"The way Wilson died ... it's very upsetting to me." Mike looked down at his coffee. "How can someone do that and then walk away without being seen? How can there be no evidence?"

"The rain didn't help," Shelly said.

Mike leaned in closer. "Do you think someone saw the killer and isn't saying so?"

"I guess it's possible, but why do you think someone wouldn't come forward if they noticed something?"

"I don't know. Fear of getting involved? Fear of retribution? Distrust of the police?"

"I can understand that," Shelly said. "When was the last time you saw Wilson?"

Mike ran his hand over his face. "About a month before he was killed. He came to my house. We played cards, had a few drinks. We got together at least once a month."

"Were there other people there?"

"Another friend, Bill Handy, and a friend of Bill's from school. Bill works at the high school."

"How was the evening? Did anyone say or do anything out of the ordinary?" Shelly asked.

One of the man's eyebrows raised. "No. We had a good time together. It was a nice, relaxing evening."

Shelly asked, "Had Wilson confided anything to you recently? Was he stressed about anything? Was he worried about someone's behavior? Did he have any difficult clients?"

"No. There was nothing out of the ordinary. Nothing Wilson said stood out. We all complain about work at times ... there's too much to do, a client or a customer is being demanding, we need a break. All just normal complaints."

"Was everything going okay between Wilson and Imelda?"

"Yeah, sure, as far as I know. Wilson never said anything about being unhappy. They seemed solid together."

"You're an attorney? What is your area of expertise?"

"Financial planning, wealth preservation, wills and trusts, probate. My office is in Rollingwood, but

I'm busy with a different venture so I'm not at the law office very often."

"You live in Paxton Park?" Shelly asked.

"In Newell, but close to the Paxton Park town line."

Shelly gave a nod. "Out of curiosity, why did you come to talk to me? Why not go directly to the police?"

"I thought you'd be more helpful. I thought the police might not be forthcoming with information because I'm only a friend, not a relative. I can't stop thinking about Wilson. I'm trying to understand how something like this can happen."

"Did Wilson ever confide in you that he was worried about his personal safety?" Shelly asked.

"Do you think Wilson believed he might be in danger?" Mike questioned.

"That's what I'm trying to find out." Shelly folded her arms on the tabletop. "Do you think he was concerned about such a thing?"

"Why do you ask? Is there anything that indicated Wilson might have had worries about his safety?"

Shelly felt they were going in circles and had the distinct impression Mike was fishing for information to see what she knew. "Did Wilson ever mention learning self-defense? Did he own a gun? Did he carry pepper spray?"

Mike stared at the young woman across from him. "I think he had some pepper spray."

"Was this recent or did he always carry it?"

"I think it was fairly recent."

"Did you ask him about it?"

"Yeah. He told me it didn't hurt to have it."

"Did he say why he thought that?" Shelly pressed.

Mike shook his head.

"Did Imelda tell you we asked her about the pepper spray?"

Mike hesitated, but then said, "She did tell me."

"So are your answers to my questions honest ones or are they based solely on what Imelda said to you? Did you see Wilson with pepper spray or are you trying to find out what I know?"

"I saw Wilson with pepper spray," Mike told her. "Imelda told me she didn't know he had it. She asked me why Wilson was carrying it. I told her the same thing I told you. He didn't really say why."

"Did your friend have any enemies?" Shelly asked.

Mike blinked. "Enemies? No, of course not."

Shelly spoke in a kind voice. "If you have some

concerns or suspicions, and you prefer not to talk openly about them, there's a police tip line you can call. You can remain anonymous."

Mike gave her a skeptical look. "Is it really possible to remain anonymous in this day and age?"

"You can tell me your concerns if you'd rather not go to the police. When I pass the information on, I don't have to report who spoke to me."

Mike gave a sad shrug. "I don't have anything to tell. I wish I did. Then maybe the killer would get caught and locked up."

"So Wilson was carrying pepper spray purely as a precaution?"

"That's what it sounded like."

"What about your mutual friend, Bill Handy? Do you think Wilson might have confided in Bill about something that was troubling him?"

Mike slowly shook his head. "I just don't know. Bill and I went to the community meeting together. He didn't let on that he knew something was bothering Wilson."

"Have the police interviewed you about your friend?" Shelly asked.

"A detective came to my office to talk to me shortly after Wilson was attacked. I think his last name was Walton."

"Did Wilson enjoy the class on finances he taught in the adult education center?"

"He did. He felt like he was helping people take care of themselves. He taught that class for years. The last time I saw him, he mentioned he was giving it up though."

"Did he say why?" Shelly questioned.

"He was tired of it. It had become a grind. It went on for twelve or fifteen weeks each time it was offered. Wilson was planning to teach abbreviated classes on personal finances at the church in town. He'd been approached by the pastor about it. Wilson was going to speak once a month or so on different topics related to the financial aspects of life. He was going to do it for free so more people could take advantage of it."

"That was very generous of him," Shelly said. "I also heard Wilson had given up playing piano at the resort restaurant."

Mike nodded. "That had gone on for years, too. He said he didn't want to be out so much. He wanted to slow down, so he cut that out of his schedule." The man glanced at his watch. "I've taken up enough of your time. I should get going." He thanked Shelly for meeting with him.

"If you think of anything that might be helpful,

get in touch with the police or you can reach out to me," Shelly said before Mike left the coffee house.

Watching him go, she couldn't shake the uneasy feeling that Mike knew more than he'd shared with her.

10

Returning home after meeting Mike Meeks at the coffee shop, Shelly spotted Juliet on the porch of her house and called to her.

Juliet hurried down the steps and when Shelly saw the look on her friend's face, she stopped short.

"What's wrong?"

"When you didn't answer the doorbell, I was about to call your phone. Jay called me. She wants us to meet her. Right now. She gave me an address. It sounds serious."

Shelly's heart dropped. "She didn't say any more?"

Juliet shook her head. "Can you come?"

"Of course. Let's go."

In silence, they drove across town, each one thinking about what might lay ahead. When Juliet turned down a country road and passed the beautiful, huge homes set back from the street, she asked, "What could be going on in this part of town?"

"Do you think they've caught the killer?" Shelly hoped. "Is that what this is about?"

"Uh oh," Juliet muttered.

Up ahead, several police cars lined the road. An ambulance stood at the end of a long driveway. A number of officers stood around talking and keeping an eye on any cars that went by.

"What's going on?" Shelly was surprised by the presence of so many members of law enforcement.

Juliet pulled the car to a stop and when the two friends approached the scene on foot, one of the officers recognized them.

"Hold up. I'll contact Jay." When the officer got off the phone, he said, "She'll be right down."

"What's going on?" Juliet asked.

"Jay will fill you in. Why don't you wait for her by the mailbox at the end of the driveway?"

Standing in the driveway, Shelly looked for a name on the mailbox, but there was only the house number on it. "Whatever is going on, it's nothing good."

Her face looking pale and pinched, Jay strode up to them and hustled the young women halfway up the driveway towards the house. "I'm glad you got here so fast. The media will show up any minute."

"What on earth has happened? Whose house is this?" Juliet asked, her eyes pinned on her sister's face.

"Mayor Daniels is dead."

Shelly sucked in a breath of air.

"The mayor?" Juliet's voice was high-pitched. "What happened to him?"

"His wife found him on the brick walkway. It seems he left his car in front of the garages and was on his way inside the house. He was hit in the head with something that resulted in severe injuries. The man is dead."

Juliet covered her mouth with her hand.

"Just like Wilson Barrett," Shelly said softly.

"I wanted you both to know about it before it hits the news. It's not something I wanted to tell you over the phone." Jay looked at Shelly. "Have you had any dreams lately?"

Feeling almost guilty, Shelly shook her head. "I haven't. I wish I had. I'm sorry."

"Don't be sorry." Jay's face took on a kind expression. "It's not something that should be forced. Let me know if you dream anything, anything at all."

"Do you think it's the same person who killed Wilson Barrett?" Juliet asked, but didn't wait for an answer. "But why? What's the connection between the men?"

A wave of dread washed over Shelly. "Oh, no. It's because of the community meeting, isn't it?"

"Why? What do you mean?" Juliet asked.

Shelly made eye contact with Jay. "You think so, too, right? The killer must have attended the community meeting. He must have heard the mayor say Mr. Barrett shouldn't have been walking in the park in the dark. He must have heard Mayor Daniels imply Mr. Barrett didn't take the necessary precautions to keep himself safe."

With a look of disgust on her face, Jay gave the slightest of nods.

Shelly let out a long breath of air. "The killer is mocking the mayor for saying those things. The killer murdered the mayor in broad daylight in the driveway of his own home."

"This guy is sick," Juliet almost whimpered. "The killer was at the meeting? He punished the mayor for what he said about Barrett not being careful enough?"

Jay put her arm around her sister's shoulders. "It's speculation. We don't know anything for sure yet."

"He's emboldened by getting away with Barrett's murder." Shelly looked at the mayor's home. "When do you think it happened?"

"About three hours ago," Jay said. "We'll know more after the medical examiner has a look."

"Did he leave any evidence?" Juliet asked hopefully.

"The scene is being processed," Jay said.

"Was Mrs. Daniels at home when it happened?" Shelly asked.

"No, she was out until late-afternoon," Jay told them. "She found her husband when she arrived home."

"The poor woman." Juliet looked like she might need to sit down.

"Was anyone at home when the attack took place?" Shelly asked. "A housekeeper? A relative?"

"No one was at home."

"So there was nobody to see or hear anything," Juliet moaned. "Was the mayor hit from behind like Mr. Barrett was?"

"It seems so," Jay said and then she gave her

sister a hug. "Why don't you take off now? The news people will be here any minute. I don't want either of you around when they show up. If they arrive as you're going to your car, cover your faces. I don't want any photos published of you here."

Jay hugged Shelly. "Go now. Hurry."

Shelly took Juliet's arm and they practically jogged to the car. Once inside the vehicle, Juliet pulled a tissue from her bag and dabbed at her eyes.

"Want me to drive?" Shelly asked, secretly hoping her friend would say no.

Juliet shook her head. "No. I'm fine. I'm not going to have you driving."

"I'm okay," Shelly protested.

"No, you're not." Juliet sniffled. "You've only driven once since the accident in Boston and you nearly passed out while doing it. You've only recently started to ride in my car without breaking into a sweat." She pulled away from the curb and headed down the road away from the mayor's house. "I can't believe this. It's got me freaked out. We were at that meeting. What if he comes after us?"

"He won't," Shelly reassured her friend. "There's no reason to come after us. There were hundreds of people at that meeting. The killer isn't going to pick us off one by one."

Juliet took a quick look at Shelly. "Why wouldn't he? He's nuts. He'll make a game of it. He'll spend the rest of his life trying to kill all of us. We'll have to be on guard all of the time."

"No, we won't. The killer took what Mayor Daniels said as a challenge. He wanted to make the mayor look stupid for saying Barrett didn't take precautions." Shelly looked at her friend. "We're safe. He has no reason to come after us."

"What if he was sitting right next to us? Or in front of us? Maybe he heard our conversation. Maybe he didn't like what we were saying."

Even though she wanted to dismiss what Juliet said, anxiety squeezed Shelly's throat as she tried to remember what the people looked like sitting around them in the auditorium.

Juliet's hand trembled on the steering wheel. "You aren't saying I'm wrong. You think it's a possibility."

"No, I don't." Shelly forced the words from her dry throat. "The killer wanted to embarrass the mayor. Mayor Daniels was a public figure. The killer doesn't care about us. Killing us would be meaningless for him."

"The way killing Wilson Barrett was meaningless?"

"The person must have had a reason to attack Barrett," Shelly said. "At least, he came up with some reason that made some kind of sense to him."

"You don't think it was a random attack?"

Shelly sighed. "I don't really know why I think so, but I'm definitely leaning that way. But at any second, I could change my mind."

"Why is this happening?" Juliet turned down their lane and parked the car in her driveway. "I hope you don't have anything planned for the rest of the evening because there's no way I'm going to stay in my house alone today. Andrew must be at the crime scene. He was going to come over for dinner later, but that must be out the window now." She turned to her friend. "Can I come in with you?"

Shelly chuckled. "Of course, you can. You know you're always welcome. Besides, I don't have any plans and I'm hoping you'll make me dinner."

"I'll make you dinner for the rest of my life as long as I don't have to stay alone."

The young women climbed the steps to Shelly's bungalow.

"Stay over. You can sleep on the pullout sofa."

"You don't have to ask me twice," Juliet said.

When the door opened, Justice was sitting in the entryway, her beautiful eyes staring up at them.

Juliet bent to pat the cat. "You wouldn't believe what's happened, Justice. Everything's going crazy. We've got a real problem here in Paxton Park."

Justice rubbed against Juliet's legs and trilled.

"She trying to comfort you," Shelly said as she plopped onto the sofa. "She's very good at picking up on people's emotions."

"She's the best," Juliet said and when she sat down next to Shelly, Justice jumped up in between them and started to purr causing the young woman to smile. "I always feel better when you're around, kitty cat."

"We can go over to your house later so you can pick up what you need to stay overnight," Shelly said.

"We can also pick up the ingredients from my house that I'm going to use to make dinner tonight." Justice had curled up on Juliet's lap.

"I'm worn out," Shelly admitted. "Maybe the killer left some evidence behind this time."

"Fingers crossed," Juliet said. "Why don't you take a nice hot bath after dinner to help you relax and then have some warm milk before you go to sleep."

Shelly narrowed her eyes suspiciously. "Are you hoping I'll fall asleep on the sofa and then you can sneak into my room and sleep in my bed tonight?"

Juliet's face was serious. "No. I'm hoping you fall into a deep sleep tonight ... and your sister visits you in your dreams."

11

The next morning, the first thing Juliet did was to ask her friend a question. "Did Lauren come to you in your dreams?"

Lauren had not appeared in any dreams that night and Shelly was feeling less than useless worrying about disappointing everyone.

"It doesn't matter," Juliet had said. "She'll come to you when she has something to tell you. Don't worry."

Shelly *did* worry and now she was feeling incapable of helping the police resolve the town murders especially since she was sitting in the passenger seat of Jay's police car on their way to interview someone who was an acquaintance of Wilson Barrett.

"I've talked with this guy before," Jay said. "He

was forthcoming and he really gave my questions a lot of thought." She and Shelly were following the walkway to the front door of the town high school where they had plans to meet with the security guard who worked evenings during the adult continuing education classes.

The guard was waiting for them in the school lobby. About five foot-eleven inches tall, the twenty-five-year-old man carried a few extra pounds, had broad shoulders, a thick neck, a round babyish-face, and dark blond hair cut close to his head.

"Officer Landers-Smyth." The guard stepped forward and shook hands with Jay. "Nice to see you again."

Jay introduced Shelly and then said to her, "This is Donald Chapel, the security guard."

Chapel and Shelly shook hands and then he led them to an empty classroom right off the lobby. "I need to start work in thirty minutes. If you need more time, I'd be glad to meet you another day to finish up."

Jay assured him the thirty minutes should be enough.

They each sat at their own desk and chair in what seemed to be a mathematics classroom since math-related posters hung on two of the walls and calculators were piled on a counter near the door. The overhead fluorescent lights were bright and harsh and caused a glare on Shelly's laptop screen as she brought up an empty document to take notes during the meeting.

Jay thanked the man for meeting with her again. "I'd like to go over some of the things we discussed at our earlier meeting. It helps to talk about them more than once as sometimes new information comes to mind."

"I'm glad to help." Chapel sat back in the chair with his hands folded in his lap.

Jay asked, "Could you tell me again how long you've been working for the adult evening classes?"

"It's nearing two full years. I also work a security job at the social security office in Rollingwood during the day."

"And how long have you worked there?"

"Almost six years. I started when I was nineteen."

"And you were familiar with Mr. Barrett?" Jay asked.

"Oh, sure. Mr. Barrett was a nice guy. He was serious about helping people learn how to save and handle their finances. I worked here in the lobby most of the time watching people going in and out of the school. The front door is the only one open during the evenings. All the others are locked. Mr. Barrett's classroom was across from this one so I could hear his lectures and discussions pretty easily." Chapel smiled. "So I didn't need to sign up to take the course. It's one of the perks of being a security guard here. I can listen to some of the classes going on."

"Did you ever talk with Mr. Barrett?" Jay asked.

"Sure. He'd get here early to set up. I'd go in and talk to him while he was getting stuff ready."

"What kinds of things did you talk about?"

"All kinds of things. Sports, cars, music. Mr. Barrett played piano. I don't play an instrument, but I love all kinds of music."

"Did you ever talk about finances?" Shelly asked.

"Sometimes. I had an account at the bank where Mr. Barrett worked. I saw him there whenever I needed to go into the bank for something."

"Did Mr. Barrett ever have a demanding student? Or did anyone ever make trouble in his class?" Jay questioned.

"You asked something like that last time and I got to thinking about it. There were a couple of minor things. One time, a guy came in drunk to his class. He didn't seem to have been drinking when he came into the lobby, otherwise I would have stopped him. He started arguing with Mr. Barrett about some point he was trying to make about investing. He stood up and went right up to Mr. Barrett, got up in his face. Mr. Barrett tried to calm the guy down. I heard what was going on so I went into the class-room and removed the guy. He never came back. Sorry I didn't think of it last time."

"When did this happen?" Jay was writing in her small notebook.

"About two months ago," Chapel said. "Maybe less."

"You mentioned there was a second incident?" Jay asked.

"Yeah, not with a student though." The guard looked down at his hands. "I didn't bring this up either when I talked to you the last time. It doesn't seem very important, but I think I should tell you about it. There's an attorney who gives a couple of two-evening classes each semester about wills and estates. One time, I was late getting here from my day job. I'm usually early so I can greet the people who teach the courses as they come in and the students who get here early. I think it's important for people to see me so they know someone is here who can help out if they need anything. Anyway, I got here later than usual and I could hear two guys arguing in Mr. Barrett's classroom." He gestured to the room next door. "I waited for a minute to see if things were going to get worse. I walked over to the door and looked in, asked Mr. Barrett if everything was okay. That lawyer who teaches the two-evening seminar was with him. They parted ways and the lawyer left to go to his classroom. I asked Mr. Barrett if things were all right and he brushed off the argument."

"Do you know what the men were discussing?" Jay asked.

"I could hear the angry voices, but I couldn't really make out the words." Chapel shrugged.

"What was the lawyer's name who was arguing with Mr. Barrett?"

"Meeks."

Mike Meeks? Shelly's eyes widened at hearing the name of Wilson's Barrett's friend.

Chapel said, "Mr. Meeks isn't here often and his assigned classroom is way at the back of the building. He rushes in and rushes out. And like I said, he only teaches two evenings each semester so I don't have a chance to get to know him."

"Did Mr. Barrett seem upset by the argument?" Jay asked.

"Not really. Maybe a little. Or maybe he was just

embarrassed by me seeing them argue. I didn't ask any more about it and he didn't bring it up again."

"And when did the argument take place?" Jay said.

"About two weeks ago," Chapel told them.

"What do you do at your day job at the social security office?" Shelly asked.

Chapel sat up straight. "Me and another guard handle the metal detector as people come in, we ask them some questions, ask them to put their phones, wristwatches, metal objects in the bins, and then we have them walk through the detector. There are some people who come in every week for different reasons. Sometimes, they get loud or angry over who-knows-what and we have to calm them down, and if they don't calm down, then we have to remove them from the office."

"Do you like working there?" Shelly asked. "It sounds like it could be a hard job."

Chapel had a proud expression on his face. "I like it. I like the people I work with. I like keeping people safe. I'd like to become a police officer someday, but it's really hard to get into the police academy."

Shelly gave the young man a smile. "I hope it works out for you."

Jay asked another question. "Did Mr. Barrett ever mention to you that he was worried about anything?"

Chapel's expression turned serious. "No, he didn't."

"Did he ever seem nervous or anxious when he was here?"

Chapel seemed to be thinking the question over. "I don't think so. Maybe lost in his own thoughts or preoccupied once in a while. I wouldn't say he seemed nervous when he was here. Except for the time that student got up in his face. I don't blame him for that."

"Do you know that student's name?" Jay asked.

"I can look it up later," Chapel said. "We have to log any incidents like that. I can email the information to you later tonight."

Jay thanked the security guard. "That would be a big help."

"Did you go to the community meeting the police held?" Shelly asked.

"Yeah, I did. It got out of hand for a while, huh? And now the mayor is dead." Chapel looked at Jay. "Do you think the killer is the same person? Or did the mayor get killed by a copycat?"

Jay said, "It's still being investigated."

Chapel made eye contact with Shelly. "That's police double-talk. It means they can't share any details with the regular public."

With a smile, Shelly nodded. "It's an ongoing case so they have to keep some things to themselves. I'm just an assistant so they don't tell me anything either."

"Did you go to the community meeting?" Chapel asked Shelly.

"I went with a friend. We left when the commotion started."

"Why? That was the most interesting part," Chapel kidded.

"We didn't think anything useful would come out of everyone shouting at each other," Shelly told him.

Jay turned the conversation away from the antics at the community meeting. "I can't recall ... did you tell me you grew up in town?"

"I grew up a few towns over from Paxton Park, but I have an apartment here now," Chapel said. "I've been living in town for a little over a year. I like the resort atmosphere. There's a lot going on." Chapel turned to Jay. "I'd really like to get hired as a police officer here someday."

Jay gave the young man an encouraging smile. "None of us knows what the future might hold."

The scent of the pine trees and the earthy smell of the soil and old fallen leaves drifted on the air as Shelly, Jack, Juliet, and Andrew rode their bikes over the mountain trails on their way to a place in the forest not many people went to see.

After locking their bicycles to some trees off the trail, the foursome hiked for twenty minutes over the forest paths and emerged into a clearing next to a cold, deep, pool of water.

For the last ten minutes, they'd been able to hear the thunderous crash as water traveled over five cascades, sped over the granite wall and boulders and down the eighty-five-foot waterfall before ending in the peaceful pool. The sight of the falls always took their breath away.

Opposite the falls and the pool, at the rear of the gorge that had formed during the ice age, a huge granite wall rose straight up from the floor of the chasm. The wall was magnificent, but it had to be respected. More than thirty rock climbers had died in the gorge over the past hundred years.

The friends stripped off their t-shirts and shorts to reveal swimsuits underneath and then removed towels from their backpacks.

"You know how cold the water is, right?" Jack asked.

"I won't stay in even for a second." Juliet lifted her long brown hair into a ponytail.

"Whose idea was this again?" Shelly kidded as she placed her towel on a rock close to the water.

"I think it was mine," Andrew replied. "And now that we're here, I'm thinking it was probably a bad one."

The day was unusually warm and the idea of a bike ride and the first, quick jump of the season into the cold, natural pool had sounded like a terrific way to enjoy the afternoon, but now everyone was eyeing the water with apprehension.

"Shall we jump in together or should we each go in separately?" Jack asked.

"Or how about not at all?" Juliet dipped her toe into the pool and pulled it out as fast as she could. "It's like ice," she nearly shrieked. "Maybe this isn't a healthy thing to do."

Andrew asked, "Should we change our minds?"

Shelly laughed. "Come on. It's always cold at this time of year. We'll be in and out in a couple of seconds. People jump into colder water than this in the middle of the winter to raise money for charity. We can do it."

With a smile, Jack said, "Okay, since Shelly has shamed us, I guess we better jump in."

The four of them stood side-by-side at the edge of the water and held hands.

"I'll count to three and then we jump," Andrew told them. "Ready?"

When Andrew reached three, they leapt into the air and screamed with anticipation as they dropped into the icy pool. When their heads popped up, they shouted and yelled and swam like maniacs to shore where they hurried out, shivering, trembling, and laughing, to grab their towels.

"That was amazing." Andrew rubbed the towel over his skin to get his frozen blood flowing again.

"I'm not sure it was amazing, but I'm glad I did it." Juliet ran her fingers through her long hair and turned her face up towards the sun.

"The amazing part was when we got out," Jack kidded his friends as he ran the towel over his head and face.

"Want to do it again?" Shelly asked with a grin and was met with an immediate loud chorus of a single word ... *no*.

Sitting on the sun-warmed boulders to soak up the rays, their skin dried quickly in the bright light and Shelly and Juliet passed around homemade granola bars they'd made the day before.

"I'd like to skip going to the police station when we get back," Shelly said. "Why don't we do it another day."

"No weaseling out of it." Andrew shook his head. "We can't put it off. We need some clues if we're going to solve these murders and every little thing we do can move us one step closer."

"It's only looking at photos. It won't be anything disturbing." Jack put his arm around his girlfriend's shoulders.

Jay had asked Andrew to bring Shelly and Juliet to the police station later in the afternoon to look at photographs taken at the community meeting.

"It *is* disturbing though." Shelly reached up and took Jack's hand in hers. "The killer was present that evening. He went to the meeting. He sat there acting like a concerned citizen. It scares me."

"It scares me, too." Juliet's sounded nervous. "What if the killer was sitting near us? What if he decided to target us next?"

"He won't," Andrew reassured Juliet. "You did nothing to antagonize him. He honed in on the mayor because it was almost like a challenge to the killer when Mayor Daniels spoke about Mr. Barrett not taking safety precautions."

Jack said, "So the killer attacked the mayor to prove to everyone that no matter what precautions they take, if he wants to kill you, he will."

"That's our interpretation." Andrew nodded and took Juliet's hand when she slipped over the boulder to get closer to him.

"That is *not* comforting at all." Juliet whined. "This nut might start picking off people who attended the community meeting to show how powerful and clever he is."

Shelly tried to ease her friend's worry even though she wasn't entirely convinced that what she was saying was true. "There were so many people at the meeting. He probably didn't even see us. We don't need to worry that he'll come after us."

"I hope you're right." Juliet's expression indicated she really didn't think her friend was right.

AFTER HIKING around the falls and returning to their bikes for the ride back to town, the two couples arrived at the police station to view the photos.

In the small conference room, they clustered around the table and stared at the pictures as Andrew removed them from a folder and passed them around.

"Scan the people in the photos," Andrew said. "See if you recognize anyone. See if anyone seems excessively eager or excited by the goings-on. Bring a picture to everyone's attention even if something looks only mildly concerning or slightly off."

The photographs of the people at the community meeting were taken from nearly every angle and level of the school auditorium.

"Who took all these pictures?" Jack asked.

"The press, the attendees, law enforcement," Andrew said. "Some were on social media. They give us a look at practically every row in the place."

Juliet and Shelly sat next to each other and stared at each photo.

"Look, here's Barrett's girlfriend, Imelda," Juliet pointed out.

"And over here is Barrett's ex-wife, Tina," Shelly said.

After a few more minutes of examining the photographs, Shelly spotted Mike Meeks in the audience, as well as some of their friends, associates, and acquaintances.

Leaning back and rubbing her eyes, Juliet asked Andrew, "Do you have any magnifying glasses? The close work is giving me a headache."

Andrew left the conference room briefly and returned with some magnifying lenses for them to use and after they had gone over all of the photographs, the detective had a short video of the meeting to play for them. "See if you pick up anything by watching the crowd."

The film showed people filing into the auditorium, waiting for the meeting to start, and the introductions of the officials. Andrew sped it up and then stopped the video right before the mayor said that Barrett would still be alive if he'd been more careful about his safety.

"Watch for people's reactions. Focus on their facial expressions," Andrew suggested.

The view panned the auditorium as the mayor spoke about safety and the crowd reacted to his comments.

"I see the security guard we talked to the other day," Shelly said and gestured to him.

Andrew stopped and backed up the tape.

"There he is. Standing right there by the exit." Shelly got up and pointed to Donald Chapel. "Oh, there's Mike Meeks, too. He moved out of his seat." Meeks was standing behind the last row of seats leaning against the wall on the far side of the auditorium.

"It was so hot in there," Juliet said. "He probably didn't want to stay in his seat anymore."

"I wonder if the man standing next to him is the mutual friend of Meeks and Mr. Barrett. His name is Bill Handy," Shelly recalled.

"We spoke with him briefly right after Barrett was killed," Andrew said. "It wouldn't hurt to talk to him again."

"What do you think about what the security guard told us?" Shelly asked. "He said Meeks was arguing with Barrett in the high school one evening. Do you think Meeks should be spoken to again?"

"I think it would be a good idea. I'll call him about having a meeting. I'll bring up the argument and see how he reacts," Andrew said.

Finishing up in the police station without noticing anyone suspicious in the video or in the photographs, Jack suggested having dinner at the resort and everyone agreed.

Heading outside into the darkness, Juliet sidled up to Shelly and whispered, "Can I sleep at your house again tonight? Talking about the murders and looking at the people at the meeting has me feeling nervous again."

With a smile, Shelly nodded. "Of course, you can. Justice will be happy that you're staying over tonight."

Shelly didn't admit it right then, but she was feeling uneasy and was thankful that Juliet would be staying the night with her.

13

J ay thanked the three people for coming and introduced Shelly and Juliet to them.

"I'm talking again with people who arrived on the scene at the park the morning Mr. Barret was found," she explained. "Shelly and Juliet were the first to find Mr. Barrett, but we'd like to hear again what you heard and saw that day."

In his mid-twenties, with an athletic build, brown hair and brown eyes, David Pillman went first. "I went out for my run and decided to go through the park. I like to run early in the morning before I go to work. When I was going up the hill, I noticed the two women." He gestured to Shelly and Juliet. "They looked concerned. That's when I noticed the guy on the ground so I went over to see if I could do anything to help out."

Jay nodded and then looked to Jean LeBlanc. In her mid-forties, she had short dark hair and brown eyes and carried a little extra weight.

Ms. LeBlanc said, "When the weather's nice, I walk through the park on my way to work at the hospital. I'm a receptionist. I saw the people standing beside the man on the ground. I thought maybe he'd fallen. I went over to see what I could do." She swallowed. "I saw the blood and got woozy. I stepped to the side to collect myself."

"Thank you," Jay said to the woman and then turned her attention to the man across from her. "Mr. Benson, would you please tell us how it was you came upon Mr. Barrett's body?"

Milton Benson was in his sixties, was tall and very slender with lots of gray showing in his light brown hair. "I was on my way to work at the town utility company. I often go through the park. It's quieter than walking on the streets. It was a very nice day. I saw the women and the jogger and then spotted the body on the grass so I walked over to see if they needed help."

"Did you notice anyone hurrying out of the

park?" Jay asked. "Did you see anyone who seemed to be in a rush?"

Benson tried to recall the day. "I don't think so. I was lost in thought thinking about the work day ahead, meetings, emails that needed to be answered. I wasn't really paying much attention to who was passing by."

"Did you notice anyone hurrying away?" Jay asked Ms. LeBlanc.

The woman blinked in confusion. "I thought Mr. Barrett was killed the night before. What would it matter if I saw someone in a hurry if Barrett got hit in the head hours before morning? His attacker would have been long gone by then."

"That's very true," Jay told the woman. "But sometimes an attacker returns to the scene to watch what's going on. So the person responsible for Mr. Barrett's death may have been in the park that morning."

"Oh." Ms. LeBlanc's eyes widened and her hand flew to her chest. "I didn't realize that. That's very disturbing."

"Do you think you remember someone who seemed to be in a hurry?" Jay repeated her original question.

"I don't know. I haven't given that any thought."

Ms. LeBlanc looked down at the table. "I'm not sure I remember who passed me that morning."

"Maybe something will come to you," Jay said in a kind voice and then looked to David Pillman. "Do you recall the morning?"

"Sure," Pillman said. "It was a warm day. The sun was coming up. I was feeling good, strong. Other runners went by me, a couple of cyclists, a couple of people walking. No one seemed to be running away from anything. The people I saw were just regular people doing their thing."

"Did any of you notice someone lurking about?"

"Lurking?" Ms. LeBlanc asked. "Gosh, no."

Pillman shook his head. "I didn't see anyone like that. Of course, it doesn't mean someone like that wasn't around."

Milton Benson said, "On occasion, there is someone in the park who looks to be a little rough around the edges, but I didn't notice anyone that morning. My mind was elsewhere."

"Did any of you know Wilson Barrett?" Jay asked.

"Not me," Ms. LeBlanc replied.

Benson said, "Maybe I'd seen him around town. He looked familiar to me when his picture was in the news. I didn't know his name though and I don't recall being introduced to him, but as I said, he did look familiar. I just couldn't place him."

"I knew who Barrett was," Pillman said. "I knew where he worked. I work at the other bank in town. I think we might have met once at a banking and financial conference, but I really don't remember ever talking to him."

"All of you live in Paxton Park, correct?" Jay asked. "May I ask how long you've lived in town?"

"Why is that relevant?" Pillman asked.

"Just collecting background information," Jay smiled pleasantly.

"I've been here about three years," Pillman said. "I moved here when I got the job."

"I've been in town for about thirty years," Benson said. "I enjoy the outdoors. I thought this would be the perfect place to live."

"Has it been a good place to live for you?" Jay asked.

"Indeed, it has. I wouldn't want to live anywhere else."

Ms. LeBlanc said, "I've lived here all of my life. I don't like the winter though. I'd prefer to move someplace warm."

Pillman looked at Jay. "Can I ask a question?"

"Yes, sure you can."

Pillman focused on Shelly and Juliet. "How did you notice Barrett on the ground? He was on the path close to the trees. What were you doing in the park?"

Shelly thought the young man's tone of voice was almost accusatory. "We'd been running. We noticed Mr. Barrett when we came off the trail."

"Really?" Pillman trained his eyes on Shelly. "I don't know how'd you'd see him from that angle."

"Well, we did," Juliet said with a touch of defensiveness.

"Do you run on the trails a lot?"

"Once in a while," Shelly said. "Not a lot." She and Juliet *did* run on the trails regularly, but she didn't like Pillman's seemingly nosy manner and didn't want to give him any information.

"Maybe I could run with you two sometime."

"Maybe," Shelly said. "Our work schedules are irregular so we kind of just go whenever we get a chance."

Benson rolled his eyes at David Pillman. "For Pete's sake, if you want to ask one of them out, just do it."

Pillman gave the older man a dirty look. "If I wanted to do that, I'd do it. I don't need your help in the matter."

Flustered, Ms. LeBlanc said, "There's no need to get angry or snippy with one another. We're all here trying to help."

Pillman flashed Ms. LeBlanc a look of annoyance and she answered him with her own expression of disgust.

"Would you prefer to be interviewed separately?" Jay asked the three of them with a stern voice. "I can certainly accommodate you by moving you into separate rooms and speaking with each person individually."

"I don't think that's necessary," Benson said.

"I agree." Ms. LeBlanc sat straighter in her chair.

Pillman pushed his hair back from his eyes. "I'm good, but if you want to talk to each of us alone, it's fine with me."

"Let's continue," Jay said. "Did any of you attend the community meeting?"

"I did, but I left when things began to devolve," Jean reported.

"That was the best part." Pillman grinned. "I stayed to watch the fireworks going on between everyone."

"I went," Benson said and then looked Jay in the eyes. "Is Mayor Daniels's death related to Wilson Barrett's?"

"How could they not be?" Pillman asked.

"I'm asking the officer," Benson pointed out.

"We're still investigating," Jay replied. "Nothing has yet been determined."

"Maybe you don't have any evidence yet," Pillman said, "but the two murders are linked. No question. What else could it be? A copycat? I don't think so."

"Why don't you think so?" Shelly asked.

"Really? It's not a huge city. How likely would it be to have two killers on the loose at the same time? No way. It's the same guy."

"Why do you think the attacker went after Mayor Daniels?" Jay asked.

"You were at the meeting." Pillman tilted his head slightly to the side. "The mayor was challenging in the way he discussed the murder. Barrett didn't take safety precautions? Really? He walked through a popular, busy park at dinner time. What precautions should he have taken? Carry a bazooka? The mayor was off-base. Lots of people thought so."

Benson's eyebrows knitted together. "Then the killer was at the meeting or he heard about the mayor's statements on the news."

"Possibly," Jay said.

Pillman turned back to Shelly and Juliet. "Did you think Barrett was dead when you found him?"

Shelly stared at the young man. "Why would you ask us that?"

"Curiosity." Pillman shrugged one shoulder. "Did you think he might be a drunk sleeping off too much booze?"

"No." Shelly bristled at the man and ignored him for the rest of the interview. *Why are there so many jerks in the world?*

14

With Justice supervising from the steps, Shelly planted some spring flowers in the bed in front of the porch. Tulips and daffodils had put on a beautiful show last month and she thought the space in front of the house should have some more welcoming blooms.

Shelly had been thinking about the previous day's meeting with the three people who had gathered near Wilson Barrett after his body had been discovered in the park and she'd been chattering to the Calico about how it went.

Justice watched the flowers being set into the soil and listened to the young woman's complaints about someone who attended the meeting almost as if the cat would give some advice on how he should have been handled.

"Some people are such jerks." Shelly gently tamped down the soil around the base of the plant.

"Who's a jerk? I hope you're not talking about me," a man's voice said.

Looking up into her landlord's face, Shelly blushed slightly hoping he hadn't heard her talking out loud to the cat. "Mr. Ballard. Nice to see you." She stood, wiped her hand on her jeans to remove some soil, and shook hands with the man.

A lifelong resident of Paxton Park, Mr. Ballard was in his seventies, had thick white hair and was slim and tanned from spending a lot of time outside. "I had to come over this way to see someone renting one of my houses two streets over. I saw you out here so I stopped. The place looks great. You take good care of it. I appreciate it."

Shelly put her trowel down on the grass. "I love the house. It's perfect for me."

"And how about the cat?" Mr. Ballard asked. "She like it okay?"

From her position on the step, Justice trilled at the man causing him and Shelly to laugh.

"I guess that means she does." Mr. Ballard reached down to pat the fine animal and Justice turned her head slightly from side to side to be sure the man scratched all the right spots.

Straightening up, Ballard said, "I wish the guy on the other street kept the house half as tended as you do."

"Is something going wrong with the house?" Shelly questioned.

Ballard rubbed at the back of his neck. "I have a lawn service for that rental because the guy said he didn't want to take care of it himself. I stopped over there because he told me the bathtub wasn't draining. You should see inside. It's like a tornado went through it. Stuff everywhere. It's a dirty mess. The guy is a pig. I'm going to have to start eviction proceedings. I'm getting too darned old for this."

"What if you give him a warning? Tell him he has to have the place cleaned up in two weeks."

"I've given him two warnings already." Ballard shook his head. "I've got twenty properties in town, some of them apartment buildings. Once in a while, I get a renter who trashes the house. It can take months and months to evict them, and then it takes a good amount of money to return the place to the way it was. I agree with what I heard you say when I walked over. Some people are jerks."

Shelly's cheeks tinged pink. Mr. Ballard *had*

heard her talking to the cat. She nodded her head and whether the landlord thought she'd been talking to herself or was having a conversation with the cat, either way, she was sure Mr. Ballard suspected she was odd.

"I need to sell some of these places. They're wearing me out." Ballard took off his baseball hat, smoothed his hair, and put it back on his head. "You have any interest in buying this place?"

Shelly's eyes went wide. She'd never considered the bungalow would be put up for sale and now she worried she'd have to find a different place to live. "Are you going to sell it?"

"The thought has crossed my mind to sell off some of the properties. I want to slow down. I'd like to spend the winters in Florida before I'm too feeble to get myself down there."

Shelly offered the man a lemonade and he accepted, and they sat on the porch step with Justice sitting right behind them.

"This cat must be good company," Ballard noted as he sipped his tall, cold, drink.

"She sure is. I'm lucky she found me." Shelly explained how Justice showed up one day and despite calling around to all the vets in the area and checking with the animal shelter and with the police, no one knew who owned the cat and no one had reported a Calico missing.

"Where'd you come from, kitty?" Ballard patted the pretty feline. "Well, I guess it really doesn't matter since the two of you found each other. It must have been meant to be."

Shelly gave Justice a warm smile.

"So what do you think? You want to buy this house from me?"

"I don't have much money," Shelly told him.

"That's a problem then." Ballard took a swallow from his glass. "You got enough for a down payment?"

"I don't know. How much do you want for the house?"

Ballard told her and then he said, "But I'll knock twenty thousand off the price because you've been a good tenant, you take care of the place, and you never bother me."

"Really?" Shelly wasn't sure what to say. "That's awfully nice of you."

"Go talk to the mortgage loan officer at Pleasant Savings Bank. Her name's Pam McFee. Tell her I sent you over to see her."

"I don't have my accounts at that bank. Mine are at Family Savings."

"It doesn't matter. If you have interest in buying the place, go talk to Pam. She'll help you out." Ballard drained the lemonade from his glass. "Think it over. Thanks for the cold drink. Shall I put the glass in the kitchen?"

"I'll take care of it." Shelly took the mug from his hand.

"Time for me to head to the next problem tenant." Ballard stood and stretched. "Thanks for not being a pain."

Shelly smiled. "You're welcome."

As the landlord headed to his truck, he said, "Talk over buying the house with the cat. She seems smart. I'll see you later."

When the man had driven away, Shelly looked down at Justice. "What do you think?"

The Calico let out a loud, happy, meow.

IT WAS A WELCOMED QUIET EVENING. After making her dinner and feeding the cat, Shelly showered and changed into comfortable pajamas, and sat on the sofa to watch a movie with Justice snoozing in her lap. When the film was over, she snuggled in her bed under the covers and read for thirty minutes before her eyelids began to droop and her head bobbed.

The cat was sound asleep next to the young woman, stretched out to her full length resting on her back. Shelly decided to follow Justice's example so she put the book on her side table, turned off the lamp, and lay her head on the soft pillow.

In the middle of the dark night, she began to dream.

Standing in a wide, green field under a bright blue sky, Shelly felt relaxed and at ease as the sun's warmth flowed over her. When she looked to the side, she saw Lauren standing in the grass about twenty yards away.

Shelly's heart flooded with love for her twin and she reached out her hand to her sister.

Lauren sadly shook her head.

The wind began to blow, gently at first, but eventually building to a near gale. The branches of the trees swayed and leaves started to fall and blow around the field.

Shelly looked up to watch as the leaves began to rip from the branches in the strong wind. With her hair blowing all around her head, she crouched down.

Lauren made eye contact with her sister and

then pointed to the sky. Dark clouds raced overhead and the air became cold, chilling Shelly to the bone.

Suddenly, the leaves turned into pieces of paper, falling all around the field, many of them hitting right on the ground in front of Shelly.

She glanced over to Lauren and saw her sister nod and gesture to the glossy pieces of paper.

Picking one up, slowly and carefully, Shelly looked at it. Then she reached for others. All of them were photographs ... some from the community meeting, some of Wilson Barrett's body, others were of Shelly and Juliet standing over the dead man as a few people watched from the side. A feeling of horror washed through her body and Shelly let the photographs drop from her hand as if they'd singed her skin.

Lauren took a few steps forward and stopped. She quickly looked over her shoulder, and then back to her sister, and then repeated the moves. Lauren ended her pantomime by using her arms to protect the back of her head, and then she stared at Shelly with a pointed expression that sent chills down her twin sister's back.

The photos swirled and lifted and rode on the frenzied air currents until they formed into a funnel cloud and then tore away through the woods with a wild roar.

With a gasp, Shelly woke and sat up in her bed, her breathing coming fast and shallow.

Justice leapt to her feet and hissed.

A bit of starlight filtered through the window into the room and with a sigh of relief, the young woman realized where she was and began to take in slow, calming breaths.

She reached for the cat and ran her hand over the soft fur. "I had a dream. Photographs filled the sky. They fell all around me. I was afraid, but Lauren was there. She stayed with me until I woke up." Shelly looked into the cat's eyes and whispered, "Lauren gave me a warning."

Justice arched her back and growled low and deep in her throat.

15

Eating chili and brown bread, Shelly and Jack sat at the small, round dining table near the big window in his townhouse apartment. The rental unit was tucked into the pine trees at the base of the mountain located only a quarter mile from the resort. A jar candle flickered in the middle of the table and its light reflected off the window.

"My landlord paid a visit to me today," Shelly said.

"Was everything okay?" Jack asked.

"He has some trouble with some of his renters. He was driving by and saw me in the yard planting flowers. He stayed for a glass of lemonade."

"He's a good guy. He keeps his places in excellent

condition and he doesn't charge an arm and a leg for the rents. I know a few people who rent from him and are very happy."

Shelly took a sip of her beer. "You know that before the accident, I had saved a good amount of money to open my own bakery?"

"I remember," Jack nodded.

"I've been working hard to save again. I work the part-time job at Glad Hill Farm and I've taken on more hours at the resort bakery so I can put money aside."

Jack had an expression of concern on his face. "Do you want to go back to Boston when you save up enough money?"

Surprised by Jack's question, Shelly sat up straighter. "No. My life is here now. I love Paxton Park. I want to stay."

Jack exhaled loudly. "You had me worried for a few seconds."

Shelly smiled at her boyfriend. "There's another reason I want to stay besides loving the town and the mountains."

"Oh? What would that be?" Jack held her eyes.

Teasing him, Shelly said with a straight face, "My friendship with Juliet."

For a second, Jack's face dropped, and then he grinned. "Is there a third reason for staying?"

With the corners of her mouth turning up, Shelly said, "There might be."

Jack leaned close and took her hand in his. "I guess coming in third isn't so bad."

Bringing his hand to her mouth, Shelly kissed his knuckles. "So I have a dilemma."

"What's that?" Jack reached for the bowl of grated cheese.

"I was hoping to one day have enough money to buy my own bakery here in town."

"That's a great idea. The center of town could use a good bakery."

"Well, today the landlord asked if I'd be interested in buying the bungalow from him. He told me he'd take twenty thousand dollars off the price because I've always taken such good care of the place."

Jack's mouth dropped open. "That's amazing. What did you tell him?"

"I have to think about it." Shelly looked down at her bowl of chili. "If I try to buy the house, the down payment will exhaust my savings and I'll be back to square one on the bakery. Again."

"It does seem like a good opportunity. Taking

that much off the house is a huge help. If he didn't lower the price, you might not be able to afford to buy."

"I definitely wouldn't be able to afford it. That twenty thousand makes all the difference," Shelly said. "It makes the down payment less and it reduces the mortgage amount I would need to borrow. It's just ... well, you know."

"You want your own bakery."

Shelly gave a nod. "But, I love my bungalow and I don't want to move out if the landlord sells it to someone else."

"Have you talked to Juliet about it?" Jack asked.

"Not yet. I wanted to hear your opinion."

"There's only one opinion that matters here," Jack told her. "Yours."

Shelly groaned. "I don't know what to do."

"Go talk to a mortgage lender. See what they say. Find out how much you'd have to pay for a mortgage on the house. If it's going to be too much or they won't give you the mortgage, then your decision will be made for you." Jack buttered another piece of bread. "And going through the process of gathering information will give you more time to think it over."

"You're very smart."

"I know." Jack bit into his bread and when a little

bit of butter got left on his cheek, Shelly chuckled and wiped it off with her napkin.

"I heard some interesting news today," Jack informed her.

"What was it?" Shelly leaned forward eager to hear what Jack had to say.

"Mike Meeks's wife is planning to divorce him."

Shelly's forehead creased. "Is she? Why? Was he cheating?"

"I'm not sure about that, but there's another frequent reason for breakups."

"Money?"

"Meeks has been trying to get his software company into the black. He's been losing money. He's borrowed too much and now he can't get any more loans. His wife is furious that he used up all their savings and has taken on so much debt. She's had enough and will be filing for divorce soon."

"Wow." Shelly looked confused for a moment. "I thought Meeks did financial planning, not software."

"He did financial planning for years then he got the idea to develop software and apps for people to use to keep track of their finances and plan for the future," Jack explained. "It started off pretty well, I understand, then the business hit some revenue issues. It sounds pretty certain the company will go under. Meeks is a wreck."

"This is a fairly new development?" Shelly questioned.

"Six months, maybe a little longer."

"How did you find out?"

"My buddy's girlfriend has been friends with Mrs. Meeks for years. They're very close."

"Meeks had an argument with Wilson Barrett not long ago," Shelly pointed out. "I wonder if it was over money. Could Meeks have asked Barrett to write him a personal loan and Barrett refused?"

"That could be. Meeks was described to me as being desperate. I can see how a loan refusal could trigger an argument between friends," Jack surmised. "Meeks may have turned to Barrett for financial help and his friend refused him."

A shiver ran through Shelly's mind. "Do you think Meeks could have been so angry that he hurt his friend?"

Jack drew in a long breath. "I'm sure it wouldn't be the first time money was a reason for murder."

"Gosh. I'd better tell Jay." Shelly's mind raced. "Wait a minute. If Meeks is Barrett's killer, why would he kill Mayor Daniels?"

"You and Jay thought the killer was insulted by

the mayor's comments about Barrett not taking the proper precautions to keep himself safe," Jack said. "Maybe the comments enraged Meeks. Meeks could be on the edge. He's losing his business and his livelihood and he's going to lose his wife, too. His life is crashing down all around him. Reality may be fraying for him."

Shelly nodded. "Meeks may not see a way out. Maybe he was with Barrett in the park trying to convince him to give him the loan, and when Barrett refused, Meeks may have gone off the deep end and in his rage, killed his friend."

"If that is the correct scenario," Jack thought out loud, "Meeks must have found something in the park to use as a murder weapon. I doubt he planned to murder Barrett."

"What a mess," Shelly said softly. When she reached for her glass, Jack noticed her fingers trembling and he took her hand.

"Jay will look into it. She and Andrew will figure it out," he said using a soothing tone.

Shelly looked into her boyfriend's eyes. "I had a dream last night."

Jack's eyes widened. "Did you?"

"It scared me." The young woman's eyes filled up.

Jack swallowed. "Tell me about it."

After she relayed the events of the dream, Shelly sighed. "Lauren wants me to watch my back. She implied that I should protect my head. My mind is warning me about someone. That's why all the pictures fell from the sky. The killer must be in the photographs we looked at when we were at the police station with Andrew and Juliet. My subconscious mind knows something. It's been able to put things together and it understands a clue." She put her elbow on the table and leaned her chin into her hand. "I just need to figure out what my subconscious is trying to tell me."

"Maybe you should look at the pictures again. I can go with you. I'll help," Jack told her. "Maybe someone in one of the photos will stand out this time."

"What if some of us are in danger?" Shelly asked with a shaky voice.

"Why would some of us be in danger?" Jack asked.

"What if the killer is afraid we're on to him? What if he thinks he needs to silence someone because he's afraid that person is getting too close?" Shelly tried to calm herself. "Why else would my sister show up in my dream telling me to watch out?"

Jack moved his chair closer to his girlfriend and wrapped his arm around her shoulders. "Every person in town needs to be careful. Everyone should be on guard. Just in case. No one knows what the killer's state of mind might be. For all we know, he may have fled the area by now. We don't know anything for sure so we all need to be watchful. Your mind is simply alerting you to the possibility of danger."

"Okay. You're probably right. We *all* need to be careful until the killer is caught. Not just me." Shelly took a deep breath. "It makes sense. Lauren symbolized my worried mind trying to tell me I need to watch my back ... just like everyone else needs to do."

"How about dessert?" Jack asked trying to lighten the mood. "I made a chocolate caramel cake. See, I'm trying to impress this baker I like."

"I bet you'll win her over," Shelly told him with a smile.

Jack brought the cake to the table, cut the slices, and set them onto the plates.

When Shelly brought a forkful to her mouth, she closed her eyes as she chewed. "Mmm. This is delicious. Maybe you need to switch careers."

"I'll think about it." A few seconds later, Jack said

with a serious expression, "Maybe think about taking another look at those photographs the police have. It couldn't hurt to go through them again. Maybe something will stand out this time."

Shelly placed her fork on her plate and met his eyes. "I was just thinking the very same thing."

16

Feeling nervous as she entered the bank, Shelly's worry was eased when the mortgage loan officer, Pam McFee, greeted her with a friendly smile and a welcoming handshake. Pam, in her mid-forties with short, dark auburn hair and blue eyes escorted Shelly into her comfortable office with two glass walls, and shut the door.

The women sat at a round, glossy wooden desk and chatted for a few minutes before Pam opened a folder to show Shelly the loan rates. As she was explaining the options to the young woman, someone tapped on the glass and they both looked up to see David Pillman, dressed in a fitted suit, peering in at them.

David opened the door to Pam's office and looked at Shelly. "Hey. It's you."

Shelly recognized the man who had met her at the police station with Jay and the two other people who had walked past Wilson Barrett's body on the morning he had been found. She wasn't thrilled to see him again.

"Do you know each other?" Pam asked.

"We've met," Shelly said. "Only briefly."

David nodded. "We met formally at the police station, but I saw Shelly in the park when she was standing next to that dead guy's body."

Shelly cringed at the young man's crude comment and Pam noticed her discomfort.

"We're going over some paperwork," Pam said trying to give David a hint to go away. "We've only just started."

"Nice to see you," Shelly fibbed.

"Yeah, you too. I'll see you." Reluctantly, David left the office and closed the door.

"Sorry about that," Pam said. "He can be a little...."

"Intrusive? Crass? Arrogant?" Shelly asked, and then was immediately sorry she showed her annoyance afraid it might make the loan officer dislike her.

"You nailed that description," Pam told her.

"Does he show those characteristics here at the bank?"

"Oh, sure, and a whole lot more." Pam made a sour face.

"I would think David would rein it in with people he works with or with people he doesn't know well," Shelly said.

"You'd think that, wouldn't you? He can be difficult. I understand he was on the scene when Mr. Barrett's body was found."

"He was. I was one of the people who found Mr. Barrett," Shelly told the woman.

Pam's face registered shock. "You poor thing."

"David showed up a few minutes after we discovered the body, but I was so preoccupied I didn't even notice him."

"No one would blame you for that. I can't even imagine." Pam shook her head. "David wasn't fond of Wilson."

Shelly stared at the woman. "Why not?"

"He held a grudge against him. David interviewed for a position with Wilson at the other bank. He didn't get it and he badmouthed Wilson any chance he got. We were at a banking conference not long ago. Lots of personnel from area banks were there. David was rude to Wilson in front of a large group of people. Wilson was presenting from the stage and David asked a lot of irritating questions and challenged what Wilson was saying trying to rattle him. The goal was obviously to undermine and embarrass Wilson." Pam narrowed her eyes and lowered her voice. "A lot of people didn't like what they saw of David that day. Our bank president had a meeting with him. David basically got demoted and warned not to make the bank look bad in the future. I'm surprised the president didn't fire him. I think he should have. You can have a dispute with someone, but that isn't the way to handle it. I was so uncomfortable at that presentation. Someone should have hauled David away by his shirt collar."

"That's really awful, but from talking with David at the police station, I can't say I'm surprised by his behavior. He even mentioned he didn't know Mr. Barrett well and couldn't remember ever talking with him."

"I'm not surprised. David has some trouble with telling the truth," Pam said. "You should have heard him after Wilson died. David went on and on about how Wilson got what he deserved. He was practically gleeful. I couldn't stand to be around him. I think David's nonsense stems partly from jealousy. Wilson was well-respected in the banking community. He was an innovative thinker, kind, concerned about making home ownership available to more people, things like that. If David was smart, he would have tried to learn from Wilson."

"Unfortunately, some people can't see what's in their best interests," Shelly said.

With a sigh, Pam returned to the information she'd started to share with Shelly, and the two sat together for over an hour discussing the costs and options of different loans.

SHELLY WAS COMING out of the bank when she spotted Jay coming towards her down the sidewalk.

"I haven't seen you in a couple of days," Jay said. "Everything good?"

"I was inside getting information about a mortgage. My landlord might be selling the bungalow and he wanted to offer it to me first."

"That was nice of him."

"I talked to Juliet about buying the house," Shelly said. "She'd love for me to do it, but she knows it's a big decision and I need time to be sure it's the right thing for me to do."

Jay nodded. "It's a huge step. I'm sure the landlord will give you the time you need to figure it out." She tilted her head to the side, and asked, "You aren't thinking of leaving Paxton Park someday, are you?"

"Definitely not. This is my home now." Shelly explained how she'd been saving to invest in her own business. "I'm torn between buying a house I love and planning for a business I'll love. Maybe I'll have to toss a coin in order to make the decision."

"Oh, gee." Jay chuckled. "Don't resort to a coin toss. Spend some time thinking it over. You'll come to the right choice."

They walked along the sidewalk until they came to Jay's car.

"You have some time to drive around with me?" Jay asked. "I'd offer to buy you a coffee, but I'd prefer to talk in private."

"Sure."

Shelly got into the car and Jay pulled away from the curb and onto Main Street.

"I was going to call you." Jay headed for a quiet, scenic road that would loop around back into town. "But before I share some new information, have you had any dreams?"

Shelly said, "I was going to call you, too. I did have a dream, but now that I've thought it over, I don't think it means anything." She reported the details of her latest dream.

Jay glanced over to the young woman. "I think it would be a good idea for you to come to the station one day soon and take another look at the photos."

"I will. Maybe I missed something earlier."

"And I think you have to take your sister's warning seriously," Jay said. "Watch your back. And your head. We all need to be aware of our safety especially since the killer's modus operandi is to sneak up behind a person and whack him in the head. It's hard to defend yourself in an attack like that. Listen for footsteps, watch for shadows."

"We can't let our guard down," Shelly agreed with Jay's comments. "Has something happened? What did you want to share with me?"

Jay carefully turned the wheel of the car to follow the curves in the road. "There's a new interesting twist in the case."

"Oh?" Shelly felt a shiver run over her skin.

"You know Wilson Barrett's ex-wife, Tina. We interviewed her several days ago. Well, Barrett never changed his will after they divorced. His entire estate goes to Tina."

"Really?" Shelly shifted a little in the passenger seat to better see Jay's face. "Is it a large estate?"

"It seems Barrett took his own advice about personnel finances," Jay told Shelly. "He saved and invested, and the money he accumulated along with the equity in his house added up to an estate worth just under three million dollars."

"What?" Shelly's voice was loud. "That much? Why in the world didn't he change his will?"

"The answer to that died with him," Jay said. "Maybe he was busy and kept putting it off."

"I don't know. A man like Barrett? I don't think he's the type to put off something like that especially since he was careful and clever to manage his money to three million dollars."

"So what are you thinking?"

"I'm thinking Mr. Barrett wasn't quite ready to change his will. He shared years with Tina. He may still have had a soft spot for her. He didn't have any other family except his father who is in a nursing home. From what we learned from his girlfriend, Imelda, she and Mr. Barrett seemed to have a committed relationship. Maybe Mr. Barrett needed more time to be sure the relationship would last before he changed his will."

Jay let out a long breath of air. "If I was the girl-friend, I wouldn't be too happy about Barrett's estate going to the ex-wife. I'd feel like it was sort of a slap in my face."

"Yeah," Shelly agreed. "But Imelda must have known what he was like, careful, methodical. They weren't married. She probably didn't expect to be in his will. At least, not yet."

"Good points," Jay said. "So do any relevant questions pop into your mind?"

Shelly's face scrunched up in thought, and then a lightbulb went off. "One in particular comes to mind."

"Yes?" Jay kept her eyes on the winding road.

"Did Tina Barrett know she was the beneficiary of Wilson Barrett's estate, and if she did, when did she discover this fact?" Shelly corrected herself. "Actually, that was two questions. Here's a third one ... did Tina know the size of Barrett's estate?"

"Three excellent questions ... and the answers to them could prove very interesting."

17

While on their way to see Mike Meeks's wife, Jennifer, Jay told Shelly about her latest meeting with Barrett's girl-friend, Imelda Wallace.

"Ms. Wallace knew Wilson hadn't changed his will, but she admitted she hadn't changed hers to include Wilson either. She regrets now that they never got around to doing it. She said it wasn't so much missing out on the money that bothered her, but the fact that Tina Barrett would receive Wilson's estate. Tina had hurt Wilson and even though they were cordial with one another, Wilson did not care for the woman."

"It's a shame that Mr. Barrett didn't remove Tina from the will," Shelly said. "I changed mine when I lost my sister. I don't have any other relatives so, for now, I'm leaving anything I have to charities."

"You were proactive," Jay acknowledged. "It was a smart thing to do."

"I've read some horror stories about people who died without wills and what happened between their family members. I'd rather have things spelled out and crystal clear."

"A good idea." Jay parked the car in front of a high-end townhouse. "Mrs. Meeks lives in some fancy digs."

"She sure does." Shelly admired the landscaped grounds and the handsome townhouses surrounding a treed common area.

Jennifer Meeks, a successful insurance company executive, opened the door to her visitors and greeted them. She was about five feet six inches tall, slender, and attractive with big blue eyes and shoulder-length blond hair. Wearing beige slacks, fashionable shoes with small heels, and a white, starched shirt, Mrs. Meeks led them into a beautifully furnished living room.

"Please call me Jennifer." She offered water, seltzer, tea and coffee and returned to the room with the beverages.

Jay began the interview. "As you know, we're

investigating the death of Wilson Barrett and are speaking with people who knew him. We understand your husband, Mike, was a friend of Mr. Barrett's."

"Wilson and Mike had been friends for a long time. Wilson was a nice person. Sort of a gentle soul, kind, smart, a good listener. He valued his friends. He enjoyed his work. He had a girlfriend he'd been seeing for a couple of years. I met her a few times."

"We were sorry to hear that you're planning to file for divorce from Mike," Jay stated.

Jennifer blew out a breath. "That's right. Things change. It's time we moved on from one another."

"How is your husband taking the decision?"

Jennifer's jaw set. "Poorly, but he'll have to get used to it because it is going to happen."

"My I ask why?" Jay questioned.

"Mike is losing his business. He blew through a lot of our money. I started to move some of it to my own account so he couldn't get his hands on it and completely ruin us." Jennifer shook her head with a look a disgust. "I told him so many times to abandon the business, but he wouldn't give up. He didn't care if he bled our savings dry. I wasn't going to lose everything we'd worked so hard to build. I think Mike lost his common sense a few years ago."

"What caused him to do so?"

"His fanatical devotion to keeping that company going."

"He created a software business?" Shelly asked.

Jennifer nodded. "The software was to help keep track of personal finances. It didn't take off like he'd hoped, but he would not give up on it."

"We heard from someone that Mike had argued with Wilson at the high school when they were teaching adult education classes," Jay said. "Had Mike and Wilson not been getting along?"

"What kind of an argument was it?" Jennifer eyed the police officer.

"Some sort of disagreement. Details are fuzzy."

"Who told you there was an argument?"

"Someone who works at the evening adult education classes," Jay said.

Jennifer let out a long sigh. "Although I didn't know there was an argument, I'm not surprised. Mike and Barrett's friendship had been strained for a while. When I turned off the cash spigot, Mike went crying to Wilson for a loan. Honestly, I was furious. He had no business trying to access Wilson's money."

"Did Mike know how much money Wilson had?" Shelly asked.

"He knew Wilson was a saver, an investor. I'm pretty sure Mike knew the value of Wilson's estate since he'd been advising him for years. Wilson was careful about money. He wasn't a risk taker. He was conservative about his spending. Wilson was very concerned about having enough to live on after he retired." Jennifer made a sour face. "Unlike Mike."

"Did Wilson give Mike a loan?" Jay questioned.

"He did. The fool." Jennifer shook her head slowly back and forth. "He didn't get the funds back. Mike ran through the money, and then had the nerve to go back to Wilson for more."

"Did Wilson give Mike a second loan?" Shelly asked.

"He didn't, no. He smartened up. Give Mike some money and you'll never see it again."

"Did Mike tell you Wilson wouldn't give him another loan?"

"No," Jennifer said. "Mike didn't know I knew what he'd done. He kept pretending to me that things were weeks away from turning around for the better. They never did. Things just kept going down the tubes."

"Bankruptcy is in the future?" Jay asked.

"It is, but Mike isn't going to take me down with

him." Jennifer crossed her arms over her chest. "I'm done with him."

"Was this kind of behavior unusual for Mike?" Shelly asked.

Jennifer thought about the question. "Mike had always been someone who had a lot of ideas. In the past, he was more cautious. He'd back away from a business idea or plan if it seemed like it was too risky. This time though, it was as if this financial software thing was Mike's last chance to make it big. I didn't understand why he felt like that. He's only in his late-fifties."

"Did you give your husband an ultimatum?" Jay asked.

"I sure did. He was burning through money like a wild fire. I sat down with him and discussed my worries. Our nest egg was in jeopardy. We're still paying off our two daughters' education loans. Mike's wild spending had to end. I suggested he bail on this venture and some day in the future, he could try again. My concerns fell flat. Mike went on and on about how things would turn around soon." Jennifer sighed. "I thought I was listening to a mad man. That was it for me. Well, not exactly. The final nail in the coffin didn't come until a little while later."

"What happened?" Jay asked.

Jennifer looked down at the floor for a while and Shelly didn't think she was going to reply. The woman's eyes met Jay's. "Mike was seeing Wilson's ex-wife, Tina Barrett."

Shelly couldn't keep her eyes from widening. This was a revelation she wasn't expecting.

"Tina and Mike had been seeing each other years ago," Jennifer said. "Wilson found out. They didn't have any kids. He offered to go to counseling, but Tina refused. She wanted a divorce so that was the end of that. I wanted to divorce Mike, but we had two little kids. I told him I'd stay, but if he ever cheated on me again, I'd be gone in a flash. Well, twenty years later, he did it again, and with the same person. How stupid am I?"

Jay and Shelly sat quietly. What could they possibly say to that?

"Mike and Wilson remained friends? Even after Mike had an affair with Wilson's wife?" Shelly asked.

"Things were strained for a quite a while. Over time, Wilson forgave Mike. Wilson admitted to me a few years after the break-up with his wife that ending his marriage to Tina was the right thing to do for both of them." Jennifer added, "Maybe Mike was desperate to have a business success to impress Tina. Maybe she was losing interest in him because he was struggling. Have you met her? She won't be winning any awards for nicest person of the year, that's for sure."

"Did Mike know that Tina was a beneficiary of Wilson's estate?" Shelly questioned.

"Was she?" Jennifer tilted her head to the side. "I don't know if Mike knew that or not, but he must have." She narrowed her eyes. "How interesting. Did Tina know she was the beneficiary?"

"We don't know. It's being looked into," Jay informed the woman.

"Oh, my." Jennifer's shoulders drooped and her hand covered her heart. "Did those two join forces to kill Wilson to get his money?"

Jay sat up. "We don't have any information that points to that."

"Poor Wilson." Jennifer's voice was soft. "I can't believe this. I thought *I* had suffered the ultimate deception."

Jay spoke up with a firm voice. "There's no reason to believe Mike and Tina conspired to get rid of Wilson Barrett. There's absolutely no evidence that points to such an idea. If anyone suggests such a thing, it would be pure and simple speculation, and only speculation. We deal in facts and evidence. We have none. Nothing at all suggests Wilson knew his attacker."

"I hope as the investigation goes on, that remains true." Jennifer's lips were thin and tight. "I would hate to have to tell our daughters that their father is a murderer."

Before arriving at Jennifer Meeks's home, Shelly would never have pointed a finger at Mike Meeks for the death of Wilson Barrett, but now, hearing about the man's obsession with keeping his new company afloat despite endangering his family's finances and finding out he'd had an affair with Tina Barrett ... twice, Mike was beginning to look as if he could be guilty. Adding in the possibility that Tina knew she was the beneficiary of Wilson's three-million-dollar estate didn't shine a very positive light on the couple.

If it turned out to be true that Mike and Tina planned and executed Wilson's murder, it would be a terrible and heart-breaking deception by two people Wilson had once trusted.

Shelly felt ill at the thought of it.

18

After work, Shelly and Juliet had time for a long walk before meeting Jay, but they chose not to walk on the wooded trails preferring to stay where lots of people were around.

"I know I'm being silly," Juliet said, "but I'm feeling uneasy about being in more isolated places. I'd rather walk or jog around town, at least until this killer is caught."

"I feel the same way," Shelly admitted. "Why take a chance? And anyway, I wouldn't enjoy the exercise because I'd be looking over my shoulder every few seconds. I wouldn't be able to relax at all."

"So now Mike Meeks and Tina Barrett are suspects?" Juliet asked with a frown on her face.

"Not necessarily, but there's some concern and

Jay wants to look into it further. It's an idea that needs more investigation."

"What's wrong with people?" Juliet demanded. "Even if they aren't the killers, getting involved with each other twice is an outrage. How selfish those two are. They completely ignore the effect their affairs have on others. Mike was married to Jennifer both times he started seeing Tina. Tina was married to Mr. Barrett the first time she started the affair with Mike and she knew he was a married man." Juliet shook her head in disgust. "I'm glad Jennifer Meeks is filing for divorce. How much can she be expected to take from that guy?"

"I'm sort of dreading going to talk to Mr. Barrett's other friend," Shelly admitted. "I hope he's not another Mike Meeks, and I certainly don't want to talk about Mike Meeks's bad ways."

"Sit and listen then. You don't have to ask questions. Don't feel pressured to take part in the conversation," Juliet suggested. "Just take it all in and see if any ideas come of it. Or any dreams."

Shelly changed the subject. They'd be meeting Jay in an hour and a half to head to see Barrett's other friend, Bill Handy, and she wanted the time outside with Juliet to be crime-talk free. "There's a place in the center of town that's available to lease. I know the space. I think it could work well for a bakery."

"Oh, that's exciting." Juliet smiled. "Let's go walk by."

The available shop was located a block from Main Street on a pretty street lined with different stores and cafes. It was empty and the big front windows were covered over with brown paper, but part had come loose and the young women were able to peek inside.

Juliet shaded her eyes and pressed her face up to the glass. "It looks great. There's a good amount of space to put tables and chairs and the counter that's already set up would work well for a bakery counter." She leaned back from the window. "What do you think? Are you going to ask to see it?"

"I think I should," Shelly said. "But it's a lease situation and I really hoped to buy a building. It makes me feel more secure to own a place. If I build up a clientele and then lose my lease for some reason, it could be like starting all over again."

"That's a good point." Juliet looked up and down the lane. "This is a really great spot though."

"I know," Shelly groaned. "A few days ago, I hadn't been approached about buying the bungalow and this place hadn't come up for lease. Now I have too many options and I don't know what the right thing is to do."

Juliet put her arm through Shelly's and they started back towards Main Street. "You'll figure it out. Of course, I'd love for you to buy the house next door to me, but you owning a bakery in town would mean I get free desserts and coffees."

Wait a minute," Shelly protested. "I never said anything about free stuff. I have to pay my lease, you know."

"I'm teasing you. I don't expect free coffee." A grin spread over Juliet's face. "Just a free dessert once in a while."

"Maybe I should just buy the house," Shelly said. "I'd miss seeing Henry and Melody at the diner every day and I would have to give up my part-time job at Glad Hill Farm. I'd miss talking to Dwayne."

"You could always visit those people," Juliet suggested.

"It wouldn't be the same."

"Think it over. There's still time before you have to make a decision. Try not to stress. Whatever choice you make will be a good one."

JAY, Shelly, and Juliet sat in white rocking chairs on Bill Handy's wide front porch. Bill was in his late-fifties, had brown hair that showed no sign of gray, and had the thin build of a long distance runner. He had a friendly, relaxed manner that set people at ease.

"How long have you taught at the high school?" Jay asked.

"Over thirty years."

"You could retire, couldn't you?"

"I could, but then I wouldn't know what to do with myself." Bill chuckled. "I really enjoy working with the kids. I think they keep me young."

"Can you tell us about your friendship with Wilson Barrett?"

Bill swallowed hard. "I can't believe Wilson is gone, and under such cruel circumstances. When I go to bed at night, I think of him lying out there in the park in the rain, in the dark, alone, hurt, injured. It's just too terrible." He ran the back of his hand over his eyes. "I met Wilson in that park over thirty years ago. We joined the town softball team on the same day. That was a lot of fun. We played on the team for about fifteen years. Life was busy, there were a lot of young guys joining the team. We had a good run, but it was time to give it up."

"You stayed in touch though," Shelly said.

"Oh, we sure did. We got together about twice a month, at least. Had dinner, got a few drinks, went skiing together, watched sports, played pool or badminton at the pub. Sometimes, I went to the resort to listen to Wilson play piano."

"Mike Meeks was a friend of yours and Wilson?" Jay asked.

"Yeah. The three of us got together a lot."

"Did the three of you still meet up together?"

"Yeah, we did. Well, maybe not as much as before," Bill said.

"Why not?" Juliet questioned.

"Mike got real busy. He started a software company a while back and spent a lot of his time with that. Wilson and I still got together regularly."

"We've heard that Mike was under a good deal of financial pressure." Jay balanced her small notebook on her knee.

Bill took in a long breath. "Yes, he was."

"He was close to losing the company?"

Bill nodded. "That's true."

"Did Mike ever ask you for a loan?" Jay asked.

A frown formed over Bill's face. "He knew I didn't have money to lend out. I make a nice salary, but I'm cautious with my savings. I don't want to run out of money as I age and I want to be able to help my kids if they need something. Wilson and I shared the same philosophy about money."

"We've heard that Mike asked Wilson for a loan," Jay reported. "Were you aware of that?"

"Yes. Wilson had a generous heart. If a friend needed help, he gave it."

"But he refused a second loan when Mike asked for one."

Bill nodded. "Wilson told me he felt very bad about not being able to give Mike the help he needed. They got into some arguments over it. I didn't think it was fair for Mike to pressure Wilson like he did. I wasn't that comfortable around Mike anymore."

"Because he hounded Wilson for money?" Jay asked.

"That, yes, but Mike had become self-obsessed," Bill said. "The only thing that mattered was what he wanted. He had tunnel vision focused solely on his own goals. There were always shades of that in his personality, but it had really come out lately. I don't know what fueled it, maybe this start-up business, but he became someone I didn't really care to be around anymore."

"You pulled back from the friendship?" Shelly questioned.

"I did. Mike could never relax. He was always wound up. If Wilson or I tried to discuss what was going on with him or offer some suggestions, Mike would get angry. I didn't want to deal with it anymore." Bill ran his hand over his hair. "One night, Wilson told Mike he needed to slow down, not be so consumed with the business. Mike got upset. He told Wilson he didn't have the big bucks in the bank like he did. Mike had been Wilson's financial advisor for years. Wilson knew as much as Mike, but he wanted a professional to look over his investments as a second pair of eyes. Mike was clearly jealous of Wilson's money. He ranted about how Wilson had three million dollars and wouldn't give a loan to a friend. Mike said Wilson wasn't married and he had no kids. He didn't have anyone to leave his money to so why couldn't he give Mike a loan? One day, he asked Wilson if he'd ever updated his will."

"What did Wilson say to that?" Jay asked.

"His face turned really serious," Bill said. "Wilson stared at Mike, then he told us he had to go home, and he got up and left the restaurant. That was about a month before he died."

"Did you ever ask Wilson why he left so abruptly?" Shelly asked.

"Yeah." Bill seemed to be trying to make a decision, then he said, "Maybe you know, maybe you don't. Mike was seeing Wilson's ex-wife. Wilson and I knew what he was up to, but neither of us told Mike we knew. Wilson told me he needed to change his will. His ex-wife was still his beneficiary. If anything happened to him, he wanted his girlfriend to get his money."

Jay held her pen over her notebook. "Did Mike know Tina Barrett was still Wilson's beneficiary?"

"I think he knew," Bill said. "Every five years or so, Mike reviewed all important documents with his clients so yeah, I bet he knew Tina was in Wilson's will. The only thing was, Mike didn't know if Wilson had recently updated his will."

19

"A celebration of life, huh?" Juliet looked around the park at all the people who had assembled for a remembrance service for Wilson Barrett and Mayor Daniels. "I don't think this was the right place to have this gathering."

"I guess they couldn't come up with another place that would hold so many people," Shelly said.

Juliet shook her head. "How about the ball field behind the high school? Or the big open space behind the resort?"

Shelly shrugged. She agreed with Juliet about the location, but maybe that was only because the place held bad memories for both of them.

A stage was set up near the lake where a band

was playing upbeat tunes. Several officials were going to say a few words, a minister would give a blessing, Barrett's friend, Bill Handy, would give a short eulogy, and then Mayor Daniels's son would speak about his father. There would be poems, some readings, and songs. The planners wanted the remembrance to be a joyful appreciation of the men's lives.

Shelly and Juliet thought not having found the killer put a damper on the idea of a joyful cele-bration.

Although Jay asked the friends to be present at the service to observe those in attendance, Shelly and Juliet had planned to attend anyway to pay their respects to the two murdered men. Jay thought there might be a chance the killer would wander around the gathering to watch what he had wrought. The idea the attacker would be in the park made the young women anxious.

"I have pepper spray in the pocket of my dress," Juliet announced as she and Shelly stood at the edge of the lake.

Shelly said, "There are a lot of people around. I don't think you'll need it."

"I'm not taking any chances." Juliet slipped her hand into the pocket of her spring dress and wrapped her fingers around the small canister. "Here comes Andrew."

Juliet gave her detective boyfriend a sweet smile and a quick squeeze on his hand. Neither thought it was a good idea to show affection to one another in public when Andrew was working.

"It's nice to see you." Andrew's eyes twinkled at the brunette and he returned her smile.

"How are things going?" Shelly asked.

Andrew's expression quickly changed to one of frustration. "Same as they have been for the past week. Not much to show for our efforts."

"There are some suspects though?" Shelly wanted to know if Andrew thought Mike Meeks and Tina Barrett had motive enough to join forces against Barrett.

"No strong pointers to anyone yet." Andrew's eyes drifted over the crowd. "I'd better keep moving around."

"I'll walk with you for a few minutes." Juliet told her friend she'd be back in fifteen minutes.

A few friends came by to chat with Shelly and then moved away to walk around the park when Jack stopped to talk to his girlfriend for a little while before he had to head to work at the resort.

"It's a huge turnout. I wish I didn't have to work."

Jack took Shelly's hand in his. "I'd like to stay here with you."

Shelly told him a few details of their visit to see Bill Handy. "He seems like a very nice person, and a true friend to Mr. Barrett. He's going to speak about Wilson today during the ceremony."

"He didn't have any suspicions about who might have killed Barrett?"

"No, he really didn't."

Before Jack left, his heart-felt parting words to Shelly were the same as they'd been for the past seven days, *be careful.*

The day was perfect for an outdoor public gathering, clear and warm with a bright, blue sky overhead. Some families had brought blankets to spread and sit on. A few kids played a game of catch down near the ballfield. A musician sat at the piano on the stage and played some of Barrett's and Mayor Daniels's favorite songs.

A man's voice called to Shelly. "Ms. Taylor?"

The security guard, Donald Chapel, walked over to her. "Hi again. Nice to see you. You remember me, from the adult community classes?" The man wore jeans and a crisp blue, long-sleeved shirt.

"Yes, I remember you. How are you, Donald?" Shelly and the man shook hands.

"It's a nice day, but sad circumstances," Donald said. He had a big grin on his face which made his comment about the day being sad seem insincere. "So many people are here."

"It's a very nice turnout for the remembrance."

Donald turned his round face to Shelly. "Have you been interviewing a lot of people about the murders?"

"I only help out when I'm needed. I just take some notes and listen while Officer Landers-Smyth talks with the interviewees."

"Do you help with the analysis?" Donald pressed.

Shelly didn't care for the man's probing interest in the crimes. "No, I don't. That's police work and I'm not a member of law enforcement."

"But Officer Smyth must ask your opinion. She must want to know what you think." Donald's expression was eagerly attentive.

Shelly forced a smile. "She really doesn't. I give her my notes and she adds them to the investigative pile."

"I'd love to be hired as a police officer some-day," Donald said. "I'd love to work on investigations."

"Police work does seem really interesting."

"Are there any openings to do what you do with the police?"

Shelly sensed the security guard thought she had some influence with the department and hoped she would pull some strings for him to get hired. "I don't know. I only volunteer with the police. I have two other jobs. Why don't you go down to the station some day and ask about the opportunities they might have?"

"Maybe I will." Donald sounded disappointed with the suggestion, but it only lasted a moment. He looked closely at Shelly's face. "Do the police have any suspects?"

Giving a shrug, she said, "I really don't know."

"Why is it so hard to figure things out? The attacker killed two people. There must be some evidence to go on." The sun's rays caused some beads of sweat to form on Donald's forehead. "Maybe I should look into the deaths. You know, like those internet sleuths do or those amateur detectives who figure out crimes. I bet I could come up with something." The young man glanced around the park. "The killer must have been really clever. Not one person saw him. Not one person saw either of the victims get attacked. You have to think like the killer to catch him. I think that's essential."

Shelly thought Donald seemed almost child-like in his fascination with the police, perpetrators, and crimes. She would have bet the man spent a lot of time watching crime shows on television. "Were your parents involved with law enforcement?"

Donald turned quickly to Shelly and laughed. "Definitely not."

Because of his strong reaction and since he didn't say any more on the subject, Shelly decided not to ask any more questions about Donald's family.

Donald put his hands in his back pockets. "Maybe I'll go walk around the area where Wilson Barrett got killed and check it out again."

"Where you in the park on the morning Mr. Barrett was found?" Shelly asked out of curiosity, thinking Donald might have a police scanner due to his interest in police work and wondered if he might have heard the alert go out that day about the crime scene and hurried over.

"Me? No, I wasn't. I wish I was. I might have noticed something. I know the murder weapon was never found. I know divers checked the lake for it, but they didn't find anything. Maybe the killer tossed it into the woods when he ran away. Maybe I'll go walk the woods for a while. Nice to see you again." When Donald headed off up the hill to do some sleuthing, Shelly noticed her landlord and his wife sitting in two of the chairs that had been set up around the park.

"Morning," she greeted the couple and took the seat next to them.

"Oh, Shelly, hello." Frank Ballard said with a smile and introduced his wife, Leona.

The three talked about the service that was about to begin, other town happenings, and how nice the weather had been.

"I saw you talking to Donald Chapel," Ballard said. "A bit of a weird-o."

Shelly's eyes widened. "Is he? Do you know him?"

"He rents the little apartment in the old Victorian house we own, right next door to our place."

Leona leaned over to speak quietly to Shelly. "He seems a little odd. I have trouble sleeping at night. I'm up quite a lot. Donald is always up when I'm awake in the middle of the night. From our kitchen sink, I can see him pacing in his sitting room, back and forth in front of his window. He seems to be talking to himself. I can see his mouth moving."

"He must have trouble sleeping, too," Shelly suggested.

"Maybe he's one of those people who only needs

two or three hours of sleep," Leona said. "I had a friend in high school who only slept a couple of hours a night. Her mother was the same way. It must be genetic."

"That could be," Shelly agreed.

"He never has a single visitor either. I feel bad for him," Leona said with a shake of her head. "I don't think he has any friends."

"How long has he lived in your apartment?"

Frank stroked his chin. "A year and half?" He looked to his wife for confirmation.

"Yes, that's about right."

"At least he keeps the place neat. Something was wrong with the faucet in the bathroom one day and he called me," Frank said. "I could have eaten off the floor in there. Everything neat as a pin. Everything in its place. He always pays his rent early. I don't care if he's a loner or stays up all night. The guy takes care of the apartment and I don't have to chase him for money. He's welcome to live there for the rest of his life."

"Or for the rest of our lives," Leona kidded her husband. "Since we've got about fifty years on the young man."

Juliet hurried over to them and sat down next to Shelly. "Sorry, I was with Andrew so long. I couldn't find you at first and then I spotted you sitting here." She greeted the Ballards and they made small talk until the service began with a number of people taking the stage.

"Did I miss anything while I was with Andrew?" Juliet whispered to her friend.

"Nothing, really." Shelly couldn't pinpoint the reason, but she felt slightly uneasy. *It must be because of the remembrance service and the lingering feelings of dread and sorrow from discovering Mr. Barrett's body.*

How she wished she could wipe that morning from her memory.

20

J ay and Shelly waited in the police station conference room for Tina Barrett. Jay had asked her to come in for a quick chat and the woman texted them to say she was running late.

"It was a nice service yesterday for Mr. Barrett and Mayor Daniels," Jay noted. "A lot of the town came out to honor them."

Shelly agreed. "I ran into Donald Chapel at the service. He's sure he can solve the murders. He's planning to spend his free time looking into it."

Jay raised an eyebrow. "I'm really not surprised. Donald is very keen on doing police work. He came in this morning to see me. He asked if there were any jobs available here that he might be qualified to do."

"He asked me about it yesterday," Shelly said. "He hoped to do what I do for you which I told him is taking notes and being a second pair of ears at interviews. I explained to him that it was strictly a volunteer position."

"I told him the same thing," Jay said. "I pointed him to the dispatch office. They have an opening for a part-time emergency dispatcher. I told him he'd have to go through training if he was offered the job. He seemed very eager about it."

Shelly smiled. "I'm not surprised. I think he'd love doing that job. He'd get all the news about what was going on in town."

The intercom in the room crackled and the man from the front desk spoke. "Officer Smyth? Tina Barrett is here to see you. Shall I have someone walk her down?"

"Thank you, yes." Jay gave Shelly the eye. "I'm looking forward to hearing what Ms. Barrett has to say."

Tina appeared in the doorway wearing a crisp business suit, her hair and makeup done to perfection.

Jay stood to invite her in to take a seat. "Thanks for meeting with us."

Looking like a fish out of water, Tina wore a

flustered expression as she hurried to sit at the scuffed conference table where she said hello to Shelly.

"I know why I'm here," she announced. She sat ramrod straight.

"Oh?" Jay sat down opposite the woman.

"It's about Wilson's will. It's about the inheritance." Tina's eyes flicked from Jay to Shelly.

"Why do you think we want to talk about that?" Jay asked.

"I'm not stupid, Officer Smyth," Tina said. "The police must think I murdered Wilson for his money. How on earth would I do that? He was taller than me. He was bigger. How could I smack him in the head hard enough to kill him?"

"No one is accusing you," Jay told her with a gentle tone of voice.

"Not yet." Tina smoothed her hair with her hand. "But you will. I didn't do it. I couldn't do it. I'm not strong enough to kill a man."

Jay said, "We're only following up with many of the people Wilson knew. May I ask where you were on the evening Wilson was killed?"

"Oh, for heaven's sake." Tina's hand went to her throat. "Why would you ask that if you weren't about to accuse me?"

Shelly noticed a few tears gathering in the corners of Tina's eyes.

Jay tried to reassure the woman. "Really, Ms. Barrett. It's simply protocol to ask such questions. You aren't the only one we're speaking with. Please keep in mind that we're trying to find Mr. Barrett's killer. Your answers may help us find that person."

Shelly admired the way Jay could usually calm an interviewee with her choice of words and her easy, non-threatening manner.

"What was the question?" Tina asked.

"Can you tell us where you were that evening?"

Tina squeezed her hands together. "I was at the office. I had reports to finish. I was in my office until about 9pm."

"Was anyone else in the office at the time?" Jay asked.

"Um. The receptionist was there until around 6pm. My two colleagues went home around, oh, I don't know, maybe between 6 and 6:30pm."

"So you were alone in the office from around 6:30 to 9?" Jay clarified.

"Uh huh," Tina mumbled.

"Did you know you were the beneficiary of Wilson's will?"

Tina's eyes went wide. "No, I didn't know that. I

had no idea. Why didn't he change it? We divorced twenty years ago. He had a new girlfriend." The woman put her hands flat on the tabletop. "I *did* not kill Wilson." Tina muttered under her breath. "But I would like to kill him for putting me in this position."

"Are you seeing anyone?" Jay asked.

Tina's eyes flew to meet Jay's. "What's that supposed to mean?"

"It doesn't mean anything. I'm simply asking if you're dating someone."

"No, I'm not." Tina's used a defensive tone and pouted. "It's really none of your business."

"When someone is murdered then a lot of things that don't seem like my business, become my business." Jay paused for a moment. "Did you know Mayor Daniels?"

"What? I met him a few times at business conferences, and at a charity thing. It was casual. I wouldn't say I knew the man."

"Had you ever been to his house?" Jay asked.

"Never."

"Have you been seeing Mike Meeks?"

Shelly was impressed with how quickly and skillfully Jay was changing the subject in an effort to throw Tina off balance.

"Mike? No, that's ridiculous."

"We've heard from several sources that you and Mike have been seeing one another," Jay said.

Tina's face turned hard. "Your sources are wrong. We're friends."

Jay went on to the next question like she hadn't heard Tina's answer. "You don't date? Even occasionally?"

"No, we don't. We're friends." The woman emphasized the last sentence.

"I understand Mike borrowed some money from Wilson Barrett."

"I don't know anything about that." Tina crossed her arms over her chest.

"Do you know anything about Mr. Meeks's software company?"

"I know he has a business that produces software to track personal finances."

"And how is his business doing?" Jay asked with an even tone.

"I don't know. Fine, I assume."

"He isn't in any financial peril?"

Tina seemed to be approaching the end of her ability to remain civil. "Why don't you ask him?"

"I will," Jay informed her. "But I'd like your opinion as well."

"Anything Mike and I discussed about his business, if anything, would have to remain confidential. If Mike asked me for advice, I'm not at liberty to discuss a client's information."

"So Mike Meeks is a client of yours?"

"I don't think I have to answer that question," Tina huffed.

In Shelly's opinion, Tina was becoming exceedingly unlikable.

"So you were in your office until around 9pm on the evening Mr. Barrett was attacked?" Jay asked.

"That's right."

"And the office was empty during the time you worked from around 6:30 to about 9pm?"

"Correct."

"You have no one who could corroborate your statement that you were there in the office?"

Tina's shoulders sagged. "No." Her voice was almost a whisper, then suddenly Tina straightened. "Wait. I ordered something from the sandwich shop on Main Street."

"Did you go to pick it up?" Shelly questioned.

"No. They delivered it."

Jay cleared her throat. "What time was it when the food was delivered to you?"

"I don't know. Around 7pm maybe. The sandwich shop delivery guy saw me at the office. Ask him. I couldn't possibly have had time to pay the man for my order and run to the park to hit Wilson in the head."

Jay and Shelly exchanged a glance.

After a few more questions, the interview ended and the woman left the room.

"The delivery guy," Shelly said.

"I'll talk to the sandwich shop people to follow up on Ms. Barrett's claim she accepted a delivery," Jay said.

"So she's off the hook of suspicion," Shelly said.

Jay nodded. "For the actual killing of Wilson Barrett, yes. But did Tina concoct the plan with someone? And did that someone kill Mr. Barrett?"

"Mike Meeks," Shelly sighed.

"I need to find out where Mr. Meeks was on the evening Mr. Barrett was attacked." Jay wrote something down on her pad of paper just as someone knocked on the doorframe to her office.

Jay and Shelly turned to see who was knocking.

An officer stood outside the door and said, "Jay. Andrew called in. He wants me to pass something on to you. Would you mind?" The officer nodded his head in a way that indicated he wanted to speak to her out in the hallway.

"I can go," Shelly started to get up.

"Hold on. I'll only be a minute." Jay went out to speak with the officer, and when she came back into the office, her face was tight and serious.

"I need to go, but I have something to share with you. Andrew made a traffic stop. He was following someone who was headed home from his office in town. The man began to speed up when he noticed someone was tailing him. Andrew pulled him over. One thing led to another, and Andrew asked him to pop his trunk. Andrew also called for backup."

Shelly's heart beat like a drum. "What happened? Is Andrew okay?"

"Andrew is fine. He and the officers found a bloody rag in the guy's trunk. It was wrapped around a tire iron."

A gasp escaped from Shelly's throat.

"The items will be tested to see if the blood matches Wilson Barrett's," Jay said.

"Who was the man Andrew stopped?" Shelly asked, her mind in a whirl.

"You'll hold this in confidence," Jay reminded her. "It was the young guy we interviewed with the two other people who were at the park on the morning you found the body. It's the young man who works at the bank and held a grudge against Mr. Barrett."

Shelly nearly fell from her chair. "David Pillman?"

"One and the same," Jay nodded.

21

The space for lease had a big, wide front room that would comfortably fit tables and chairs near the two big windows overlooking the brick sidewalk. A long counter and glass cases ran along what would be the ordering and serving area. The coffered ceilings were high and Shelly could picture two or three chandeliers lighting up the shop.

"This place is practically perfect." Juliet walked slowly around to get a feel for where everything would be set up. "There are already glass cases here where you can showcase your pastries. It would be so nice to sit by the windows and sip a coffee or an iced tea while watching the people walk past."

Shelly glanced around at the walls. "I think I'd paint the walls a more neutral color, but other than that, this place is really great. It wouldn't take a lot to get a bakery up and running in here, but it would still be expensive to make the necessary changes."

"Let's check out the backroom." Juliet led the way into the workroom. "Oh, look. It's big. There's so much counter space to prepare the pastries and there's a huge walk-in refrigerator. Is it staying? Then you wouldn't have to buy and install one."

"I don't know. I'll ask the owner about it." Shelly took a look at the small office where a safe was located and then checked out the storage area and the bathrooms. Returning to the front room, she and Juliet sat at the one table that was left in the room.

"What are you thinking?" Juliet asked her friend.

The sunlight streamed in the through the window and shined onto the wood floors.

"I just don't know. I'm not sure what to do. Lease this place and open a bakery-café or buy the bungalow. My head is spinning."

"You don't have to do anything," Juliet told her friend. "Keep everything the way it is for now. You're happy. Things are going well. If you're not ready for a new step, then wait until you are."

Shelly grinned. "You're far too sensible."

"That's why you keep me around," Juliet kidded.

Shelly's smile faded as she considered the possibilities. "I like living next door to you. If I don't buy my house, someone else will and I'll have to find another place to live. I love the bungalow. I love the location. It's perfect for me and Justice likes it, too."

"Then maybe you should buy it." Juliet leaned back in the chair.

"You think so?" Shelly asked.

With a chuckle, the young woman replied, "This is your decision and your choice. I'm staying out of it."

"My brain is a muddle." Shelly folded her arms over the table and leaned on them. "This case has me going in circles."

"But there's a good chance it's going to be solved. David Pillman has a bloody cloth in his car wrapped around a tire iron. Once the blood is tested, it might be all over for Pillman."

"I don't know."

Juliet eyed her friend. "Did you have a new dream?"

With a shake of her head, Shelly told Juliet she hadn't had a dream since the last one when photos were falling from the sky like leaves. "No other dreams since that one."

"What good was that dream?" Juliet questioned. "The photos we looked at down at the station didn't reveal a thing. When we go there in a couple of hours to look at the pictures again, the result will be the same."

"Something new might stand out." Shelly's voice was hopeful. "We might have missed something last time."

"There were four sets of eyes on those pictures. We didn't miss a thing. One of us would have seen something if there was anything to see."

"Why don't I have more dreams?" Shelly's shoulders rounded in defeat.

"I bet you will. It might not matter anyway. Pillman might be the one."

"Was Pillman that resentful of Wilson Barrett that he would attack and kill him?" Shelly couldn't believe a small thing like not getting the job Pillman interviewed for would set off a chain of events that would end with Barrett's death.

"It seems he was." Juliet checked the time on her phone. "Why don't we leave this possible coffee shop and go to a functioning one? I could use a hot coffee before we have to go to the police station to look at those photos."

The young women left the storefront, locked the door, and dropped the key off to the real estate agent who was handling the leasing of the place, and then they headed to Main Street to get coffee and pastry at the café.

Settled into a comfortable booth, Juliet looked around. "Do you think this town can support two places that serve coffee and dessert?"

"I think it can. Lots of people love to go to a coffee shop," Shelly said. "I'm surprised there aren't more of them in town."

"Then maybe you better grab that empty shop and make a million dollars off of the coffee and sweets." Juliet lifted her full mug to her lips.

Shelly groaned. "I'm just going to flip a coin. Heads, I buy the house. Tails, I lease the shop."

"No, you are not going to flip a coin." Juliet sat up at attention. "You're going to make a choice using reasoning and logic to pick what's right for you at this time."

Shelly slumped in her chair. "You choose for me."

Juliet rolled her eyes. "We're changing the

subject now. You can leave everything to stew in your head for a while."

The friends split a cinnamon roll and sipped their drinks.

Juliet said, "Jay told me Donald Chapel is probably going to work for the dispatch center on a part-time basis."

"That guy is obsessed with police work," Shelly noted. "It will be a dream job for him. He'll know everything that's going on with law enforcement. Well, not everything, I guess."

"Enough to make him happy anyway," Juliet said.

A woman approached the table and Shelly looked up to see Pam McFee standing beside them holding a cup of coffee. "Hi. Would you mind if I joined you? The place is full."

Shelly welcomed the woman and introduced her and Juliet to one another.

Pam removed the lid to her drink and a plume of steam rose from the cup. She took a delicate sip, and then turned her eyes to Shelly. "Have you heard the latest about David Pillman?"

"What do you mean?" Shelly wasn't going to spill anything confidential about what the police discovered in Pillman's trunk. As it turned out, she didn't need to worry.

Pam leaned close. "Pillman had a rag with blood on it in his trunk."

"How do you know that?" Juliet asked.

"It was just on the news. I saw it on my phone." Pam held her cup. "I knew that guy was bad news. You could tell he was trouble, too," she addressed Shelly.

"He was rude when we talked to him," Shelly agreed. "What did the news story say?"

"Not much more than that," Pam told them. "The blood on the cloth will be tested to see if it matches Wilson Barrett's. If it doesn't match, Pillman is off the hook. I don't know what to believe about the guy. He strongly disliked Wilson. He was a jerk towards him. But it's incredibly hard to believe that resentment would fuel the hatred required to murder someone. And Mayor Daniels, too. Two men dead." Pam shook her head. "For what? Why? To prove you're better than Wilson or Mayor Daniels? To teach the men a lesson? It's a dangerous game someone was playing. I guess I hope that Pillman is the killer then everything can go back to the way it was."

Shelly didn't think things could go back to normal, at least not for some, especially the victims and their families and loved ones. Would people in town remain distrustful of others? Would parents allow their kids to go to the park without them? Would people walking alone avoid the park at dusk, and later? Would townspeople look at each other with the suspicion that something dark was lurking deep within just waiting for the right opportunity to emerge?

"Wilson was such a good man," Pam said. "It goes to show that anyone can rub someone the wrong way and if the other person's annoyance or anger or sense of having been wronged escalates, then you could be in for a big heap of trouble even though you really did nothing wrong."

"It's an unsettling thought," Shelly agreed.

"Isn't it?" Pam asked. "I had a run-in with someone not long ago. It scared me."

"What happened?" Juliet asked.

"I signed up to take a six-week French class at the adult education program that runs in the evenings at the high school. I got there early to find the classroom and parked in the first row near the sidewalk. I got out and started walking to the front door when I realized I left my wallet in the car so I went back. I saw a man park next to me and when he got out, he hit my car with his door. When I checked, there was a big scratch and a dent on my car. I asked him to exchange insurance information. He got so angry.

He said the scratch was there already. He didn't do it. It was such a simple thing. I was being polite when I suggested we share our information, but I got angry when he denied causing the scratch and dent. When I insisted he did it, the guy came so close to me. It was in a very threatening way. I was afraid. I didn't know if he was going to strike me or what."

"What happened?" Juliet asked. "Were you able to get away from him?"

"Just then Wilson Barrett arrived and pulled in next to the man's car. He noticed something was going on and approached us. Wilson knew the man. He asked what was wrong. I told him. The man denied everything, said I was a liar trying to get him to pay for the scratch when he wasn't the one who put it there. He got loud. Wilson took my arm and escorted me inside the school. He asked if I was okay. He was so nice to me. He walked me to my classroom and told me he would speak with the security guard. I told him no, not to bother, that I didn't want to have the guard talk to the man and I didn't want to have any more to do with it." Pam looked from Shelly to Juliet. "Wilson explained to me that the man in the parking lot *was* the security guard."

"The man who argued with you about the

scratch was the security guard?" Juliet asked with wide eyes.

"Yes," Pam said. "Well, I never went back to that French class. I would never feel safe with that guard there. He wasn't able to control his anger. I was nervous to be around him. The whole thing gave me nightmares for weeks."

22

Photographs were lined up in rows on the conference table in the police station and Shelly and Juliet held magnifying glasses above the pictures in order not to miss any important details.

Shelly let out an exasperated sigh and placed the magnifier on the table. "You were right," she told her friend. "There isn't anything here. Why did I have that dream of photographs falling down on me? Did it mean nothing? Am I misinterpreting something?"

Juliet yawned and rubbed at her eyes. "I think I'm going blind."

Shelly ignored the comment. "What was Lauren trying to tell me?"

"I don't think you should push," Juliet said. "Let

the dreams come as they may, or not. Either your subconscious will pick up on something or it won't. This isn't something you can force. We're not law enforcement agents. No one expects us to do any more than what we're able to do. We're aren't trained police officers. We're both good at noticing things and sometimes people reveal more to us than they do to the police, and you have dreams. But we're on the periphery of the investigation. We aren't the main investigators and no one expects us to be. Either something is there for us to notice or it isn't. We can't pull things out of the air. Jay doesn't expect us to."

Jay entered the conference room. "Have you pulled anything out of the air yet?"

Juliet and Shelly stared at the woman.

"I'm kidding." Jay gave them a little smile. "I heard the tail-end of your conversation." She sank into a seat at the table looking exhausted. "Juliet's right. I don't expect more from you than what you can do. Sometimes, you'll find something. Don't pressure yourself. It's never your investigation to solve. If you're able to find something that helps, I'm grateful, but I don't expect it from you."

Shelly gave a nod. "Thanks."

"So. As far as the information Pam McFee

shared. I made a call to the guy in charge of the adult education program. His name is Al Hood. His thing is the logistics of the courses, keeping people safe, making sure things run smoothly. He's not the one in charge of putting the classes together. Al remembers Wilson Barrett talking to him about the woman in the parking lot and Donald Chapel. Barrett reported what he was told by the woman. Al gave it some thought. He hadn't had any trouble with Chapel previously, but called him in to have a chat. He said Chapel had been involved in a fender bender earlier in the day ... he'd been rear-ended. Chapel was upset that his insurance would drop him if he had two claims in one day so he lied about not being responsible for the woman's dent and scratches. And because Pam McFee didn't want to press it any further, Al didn't think the incident warranted firing Chapel. He gave him a warning and an explanation about how he was to deal with people coming to the school. There haven't been any other issues."

"I think it should have been handled differently," Juliet spoke up. "Chapel was out of line. At the very least, he should have given his insurance information to Al and Al could have passed it to Pam. Chapel gets off with barely a slap on the hand."

"I suggested that very thing. The incident only

happened a few weeks ago. I don't know if Al will pursue trying to get the insurance information from Chapel, but I have no authority in this thing. I wasn't called to the school when it happened." Jay stretched and massaged the back of her neck. "I will pass the story on to the manager of the dispatch center. He may think twice about hiring Chapel if the young man isn't able to control his temper." Jay looked down at the photos on the table. "How about all this? Did you have any luck?"

"None." Suddenly, Shelly felt a wave of fatigue wash over her and she wanted to crawl into bed with Justice beside her and pull her blanket over her head.

Jay said, "I checked with the sandwich shop in town that Tina Barrett reported to have ordered dinner from on the evening Barrett was killed. She was telling the truth. She paid with a credit card and they had her information on record. They also had the details of which of the drivers delivered the meal. His name is Lewis Montero and he confirmed he handed the order to someone who matches a description of Tina."

"There isn't anyone else in that office who looks like Tina so she couldn't be the one who killed Barrett," Juliet said.

"Mike Meeks is another story," Jay told the young women. "His whereabouts can't be confirmed by anyone. I requested phone records to see which towers pinged his phone on the day Barrett died. Meeks's phone must have been turned off because after 5:30pm that day, his phone isn't sending any signals."

"That's suspicious, isn't it?" Shelly asked. "Meeks just happened to turn his phone off around the time Barrett was attacked?"

"There could be other reasons for him to turn off his phone," Jay said.

"Like what?" Juliet questioned.

"Maybe whenever he visited Tina," Jay suggested. "When he spent time with her, he may have turned off his phone so no one could tie him to the same place where Tina was. People who cheat often have their phones turned off at certain times of the day. That way, there are no pinging cell towers to tell on you." She gave Juliet and Shelly pointed looks.

"Where does Mike Meeks say he was at the time Barrett was murdered?" Shelly asked.

"At home. Alone."

"Convenient." Juliet frowned.

"No one can vouch for him?" Shelly asked.

"No one." Jay picked up a photo and stared at it for a few moments, and then set it back down. "What do you think about the bloody cloth in David Pillman's truck?"

"I think it's suspicious," Juliet said.

"What does Pillman say about it?" Shelly asked.

Jay let out a long breath. "He said he and a friend were driving around and got a flat tire. The friend used the tire iron to remove the lug nuts, or I should say he was trying to remove them. They were stubborn. He yanked on the tire iron, it flew up into his face, and he got some pretty bad cuts. He required stitches."

"That must be easy to confirm," Juliet said.

"The friend did go to the hospital on the night Barrett was killed and he did receive stitches and the story they gave the doctors was the same, but how do we know what actually caused the facial cuts?"

"Oh," Juliet said realizing her error. "They could be lying about it. He could have been injured while helping Pillman murder Mr. Barrett."

"Where's Pillman's friend? Can't his blood be tested to see if it matches the blood on the cloth in the trunk?" Shelly asked.

"He's traveling overseas. Pillman can't reach him.

The friend isn't using his American phone. Pillman doesn't know the friend's itinerary."

Juliet groaned. "What a bunch of nonsense. You don't believe Pillman, do you?"

"It doesn't matter what I think. The blood on the cloth will be tested against Barrett's."

"And if the blood matches, Pillman and his friend are in trouble," Juliet said.

"Do you mind going by the park?" Shelly asked when they left the police station.

"Why?" Juliet wanted to know.

"I want to go look around."

"For anything in particular?"

"I just want to look at the area where we found Mr. Barrett."

"Who am I to object?" Juliet asked, and they headed to the park.

When they arrived, they followed the path up the hill to the place where Wilson Barrett fell from the attacker's weapon. A huge pile of bouquets and single flowers rested on the spot of grass where the dead man had been. Cards, notes, and ribbons mingled in with the flowers.

"Mr. Barrett was walking home." Shelly glanced down to where Barrett had started the climb up the slight hill. "It was dusk, almost dark." Shelly moved onto the walkway the man had been on. "Walk behind me," she asked Juliet. "Be stealthy."

The women walked a few yards along the path.

"What shoes are you wearing?" Shelly turned around to look. "Soft soles or hard?"

"Soft."

"I could hear you walking behind me. Let's do it again, but let's start further down the path."

They repeated the walk, one behind the other.

"Was it windy that night?" Shelly asked.

"I don't remember. Why does it matter?"

"The wind might muffle the sound of someone coming up behind."

"Could you hear me walking this time?" Juliet asked.

"Yes, but I guess it could be easy to miss." Shelly stood with her hands on her hips, and as she turned in a tight circle, she let her eyes wander over the area. "Do you remember the people who stopped to help that morning?"

"Not much. I know people asked me questions, but I can't really recall what they looked like or what they said to me," Juliet replied.

"Do you remember where they were standing?"

Juliet took a look around. "Um, maybe one was over there and one was right here. Is that what you remember?"

"Vaguely. I think my brain shut down when we found the body. Was anyone else around?"

"Besides the three people who asked us questions?" Juliet ran her hand over her forehead. "I'm not sure." She watched her friend as she moved around the spot. "Is there something you're looking for?"

"Yes," Shelly said. "I feel like there's a clue here, but what it is and where it is, I just don't know."

23

Shelly went to bed feeling helpless and hopeless and before trying to sleep, she read a few chapters of a mystery to take her mind off the case. Justice curled up next to her, purring loudly, and the sound slowly comforted and relaxed the young woman. After reading for an hour, Shelly turned off the lamp.

Once in a deep dream state, she began to feel as if she were floating. Shelly was at the edge of the woods where the mountain trail led into the park. She felt the ground under her feet, but she was able to move around without seeming to take any steps.

She looked to the spot on the lawn where Barrett's body had been, but there was only grass and the walkway. A cloud passed overhead and darkened the area for a few moments, and then the photographs began to fall again. Fluttering down from the sky, the pictures covered the grass. Shelly bent to pick some up and saw that each one was of people in the park.

A shadow moved behind the trees near where Barrett's body had rested. It was Lauren who stepped out of the woods, and when she made eye contact with her sister, Shelly's heart swelled with warmth.

Lauren touched her abdomen, then moved her hand to the back of her head. She glanced behind her to the woods, and turned back to Shelly. Lauren repeated what she'd done ... looking at the woods, and then back to her sister.

She stared into Shelly's eyes, shook her head, placed her hand on her heart, and slowly faded into the air.

Before going to work, Shelly called Jay and Juliet to report the dream, and when they asked for her interpretation of it, she had no answer. "I don't know what it means."

"Don't worry about it," Jay reassured her. "Something might come to you during the day or maybe Lauren will appear again to clarify your thoughts."

Shelly couldn't stop thinking about the dream. All day while she baked, her thoughts kept returning to the images in the dream ... the woods, the photos falling from the sky, the park, the place where Mr. Barrett died, her sister emerging from behind the trees, Lauren touching her abdomen and her head.

Did someone surprise Mr. Barrett? Did someone hide in the woods waiting for him to pass? Is that why he didn't seem to hear anyone overtaking him on the walkway? Was the attack premeditated? What are we missing?

"Mrs. Daniels contacted me two hours ago," Jay said to Shelly as she drove the car to a town forty minutes away. "She said she would only speak with me. I asked if I could bring my assistant along and she reluctantly agreed."

"What could Mayor Daniel's wife have to tell you?" Shelly watched the pine trees flash by as they traveled along the country road, anxiety filling her veins. "She wasn't at home on the afternoon the mayor got killed."

"No, she wasn't, but maybe she knows something that hasn't come out yet. Maybe someone made threats against the mayor. Maybe she noticed someone in the crowd at the community meeting."

"She was there?" Shelly asked.

"She sat in the front row on the right side of the auditorium." Jay turned the car into the parking lot of a small diner. "Mrs. Daniels sure picked an out of the way place. The woman clearly wants anonymity."

Heading inside, Shelly said to Jay, "Well, we're about to find out what she has to say."

Mrs. Emily Daniels sat in the back booth of the diner. She wore jeans, a blue shirt, and a light jacket. She had her shoulder-length hair pulled back in a loose bun and she wore black-framed glasses. She gestured to Jay when she noticed the police officer come in.

"Thank you for meeting me," Mrs. Daniels said after introductions were made. "I appreciate you coming all this way. My friend owns the diner. I prefer this to be a private conversation."

"I understand." Jay nodded. "How can we help?"

"I hope I can help you." Mrs. Daniels reached into her handbag and removed a phone which she placed on the table. "I found this in my husband's things. I didn't know he had a second phone. I found some interesting text messages on it." She picked up the phone, turned it on, and handed it to Jay. "Go ahead and read some of them."

Jay spent a couple of minutes scrolling through the text messages. "Your husband was involved in an affair?"

"So it seems." Mrs. Daniel's face was drawn and serious. Despite her carefully applied makeup, she looked like she hadn't slept in days. "I was devastated when my husband was murdered. Now I have some different emotions to deal with."

"Did you have any hints that Mayor Daniels was having an extra-marital affair?" Jay asked.

"I had no idea. But now, after finding this, I look back at things and realize some clues were right in front of me and I ignored them. I guess I preferred to believe my husband was honest and faithful." Mrs. Daniels's put her face in her hands for several moments. "This whole thing is a nightmare. I can't believe what's happened. I can't believe my husband was a cheater. I feel like my entire adult life has been a lie."

Shelly could almost feel the woman's pain and mental anguish.

Mrs. Daniels took a long drink from her coffee

cup. "After I discovered the phone and what was on it, I was so embarrassed and ashamed that Clay cheated on me that I wasn't going to report it to anyone. But then I got to thinking, maybe this woman knows something about Clay's murder. Maybe he confided things to her that he didn't share with me. Maybe she can be useful in helping to find the killer."

The woman forced a smile. "Not because I want justice for Clay. Oh, no, I'm not a martyr. I want justice for Wilson Barrett. He was a kind man and he didn't deserve to die, and certainly not like he did."

"I appreciate your help," Jay said. "You told me the other day that you knew Mr. Barrett professionally, that you met him at a charity event. Did you and your husband socialize with him?"

"We didn't. We did work with him on obtaining several mortgages. Wilson was wonderful to work with, so intelligent, so knowledgeable. We were very impressed with him." Mrs. Daniels looked down at the phone on the table. "Can you use the information on the phone to identify the woman who communicated with Clay?"

"That depends," Jay said. "These kinds of phones are very useful to someone who wants to go incognito, to people who wish to conceal their identities.

The phones can be purchased with cash so there's no credit card trail available. If your husband's contact used a similar type of phone, it will be very difficult to find out who she is."

"I see." Mrs. Daniel's took a deep breath. "That would be unfortunate." She seemed to be debating with herself over something. "Well, maybe I can point you in the right direction."

"Ma'am?" Jay asked. "Do you know who this woman might be?"

"It's possible. As you can imagine, I've spent a lot of time thinking about this. I won't say why I suspect it could be a particular person, but I will tell you who I think it might be, if you keep what I say in confidence. I could be wrong, and I don't want the woman to know I suspected her and reported her to the police."

"I'll keep it in confidence within the boundaries of law enforcement and will only share the information with the members who need to know," Jay promised.

When Mrs. Daniels looked to Shelly for affirmation, the young woman nodded her head. "I will as well."

"Okay then. My suspicion points to Tina Barrett. She owns an accounting firm in town."

Shelly's eyes went wide and she exchanged a quick glance with Jay.

"You must know her," Mrs. Daniels said. "She's Wilson Barrett's ex-wife."

"We've met her, yes," Jay said while keeping her facial expression even.

"That's who I think was having an affair with Clay. If I'm correct, then maybe Tina can prove herself useful in determining who the killer might be, and in doing so, redeem herself a little for what she did to me and my family."

WITH JUSTICE WEDGED in between them, Shelly and Juliet sat on the sofa with cups of tea. Jay had just left after bringing Juliet up to speed on the latest twist and discussing the many different aspects of the case.

Before leaving the bungalow, Jay had said, "I'll see about getting some cell tower pings on Mayor Daniels's secret phone. Then I'll approach Tina Barrett about her relationship with the mayor ... something I'm not looking forward to."

"Tina's a busy woman," Juliet said to Shelly while patting the Calico. "Maybe she didn't want to spend any more time on Mike Meeks since he was in trouble financially. Tina may have preferred someone more successful, like the mayor."

"I don't know where she finds the time," Shelly said. "And all the energy to keep things secret. You'd have to be careful of everything you said, making sure never to let anything slip out about who you were with and when. It seems like it would be exhausting."

"I agree," Juliet said. "There's another thing that's exhausting. Since you had those dreams about photographs floating down from the sky, I've been combing social media looking for pictures taken at the park on the day Mr. Barrett was murdered."

Shelly shifted to face her friend. "You have?"

"There's a ton of stuff to go through. I saved some of the pictures I found that could be interesting. I brought my laptop over to show you some of the ones I've saved."

Shelly was eager to see the photographs. "Let's look."

Juliet took her laptop from her big shoulder bag and turned it on. When she opened the folder of pictures, she turned the screen so Shelly could see. "These were taken by people who were in the park on the day of the murder. Some were taken right after we found Mr. Barrett's body, and some were taken at other times during that day."

Shelly leaned closer to the screen and scanned the pictures. Some showed the body on the ground. "Someone posted pictures of the body? Why? It's so intrusive."

"Some people have no sense of what's appropriate," Juliet sighed.

Shelly continued to look at the photos. "Wow, you've spent a lot of time on this."

"I don't have dreams so I had to think of some other way to be helpful."

"Wait," Shelly said. "Go back." Staring at the picture of a crowd of people watching the police secure and process the crime scene, she noticed someone familiar.

"Look here." She pointed. "This guy in the back. See him? It's Donald Chapel, isn't it?"

Juliet took a close look. "You're right. It is him, the security guard."

Shelly turned to her friend. "Donald claimed he wasn't in the park that day. I specifically asked him about it. He lied to me."

24

Thinking over why Donald Chapel would lie to her about being in the park the morning Wilson Barrett's body was found got Shelly wondering who else might be lying to them. When she finished baking in the diner's kitchen for the day, she rode her bike from the resort to the center of town and stopped into the popular sandwich shop. Shelly ordered a hummus and vegetable wrap and took a table by the window. While she ate, she watched two of the shop's delivery people coming and going, and when she was finished eating, she approached the counter.

"Is Lewis Montero working today?" she asked.

The man behind the counter looked up at the clock. "Lewis will be here in about fifteen minutes."

Shelly waited at the table until the young man arrived for his shift. The man behind the counter pointed Shelly out and said a few words to the delivery driver.

Lewis eyed her, and walked slowly over to the table.

"I'm Shelly Taylor. Do you have a couple of minutes?"

"For what?" About twenty-years-old, Lewis was tall and slender with light brown hair and dark eyes. He wore jeans, a t-shirt, and a jean jacket.

"I just want to talk. I need to ask a few questions about something."

"You a cop?" Lewis looked at her warily.

"No, why? Did you do something wrong?" Shelly asked.

"No, I didn't." Lewis's tone was cheeky.

"I'll be glad to pay you for your trouble." Shelly put a small stack of twenty-dollar bills on the table.

Lewis looked at the money, moved his eyes to Shelly, and sat down scooping up the bills from the tabletop. "Make it quick. I gotta clock in to my shift."

"A police officer talked to you recently about a delivery to T.B Accounting. It was in the evening. You delivered food to a woman who worked at the business. Do you remember?"

"Do you mean do I remember making the delivery or remember talking to the cop?" Lewis sat back in his seat.

"Either. Both." Shelly watched the man's face.

"Yeah."

"To making the delivery or talking to the officer?"

"Both."

"Can you describe the woman you delivered the food to?"

"Dark reddish hair, thin, average height. She had on a suit. She talked fast. I gave her the bag, she gave me a tip, and I left."

"Did she say anything to you?" Shelly asked.

"Thank you?" Lewis said. "We didn't have a conversation. She wanted her food and I wanted to make another delivery."

"What did she order?"

"I don't know. I don't remember. Who cares?"

"What time was it when you made the delivery?"

Lewis sighed. "I only know because that cop asked me the same question. It was a little before or a little after 7pm. Why's everyone so interested in this woman's eating habits?"

"Because we've got nothing better to do," Shelly said. "Are you sure you were there at 7pm? You know if you lied to that officer, you'd be in trouble, right?"

Lewis leaned across the table. "I didn't lie."

"Did you get the time right? Could you be wrong about the time?"

"I don't think so."

"Did anyone ask you to tell people who asked about the time that you were there at 7pm?"

"No."

"Were you there a little earlier maybe?"

"What? Like five minutes?"

"More like an hour earlier," Shelly said.

"No."

"You sure?"

"I'm positive. Look I gotta go to work. Why are you asking this stuff anyway? I told the cop the same stuff."

Shelly folded her arms onto the tabletop. "Because lately, I don't believe everything I'm told."

Lewis got up and went into the backroom, and in a few minutes, came out wearing a shirt with the sandwich shop logo on it, picked up some items packaged for delivery, and headed for the door. He nodded to Shelly as he walked past.

From the window, she watched him get into his car, but before he drove away, Lewis put his phone to his ear and spoke into it, taking an occasional glance at the store while he talked.

Shelly wondered who he might be speaking to.

OUTSIDE AT THE BICYCLE RACK, Shelly unlocked her bike. Feeling annoyed about the exchange with the delivery driver, she wasn't sure if he was lying to her or not and she wondered if the call he made when he got into his car had something to do with her and her questions.

Someone called her name and when she looked up to see Donald Chapel coming towards her, her heart dropped.

Donald gave her a friendly greeting.

"What are you doing in town?" Shelly asked.

"I went by the police station. Officer Smyth wasn't there. I'm applying for a dispatcher position. I wanted to ask how things were going and when I'd find out if I got it."

"Oh, that's good." Shelly could feel her blood begin to boil because Donald lied to her about not being in the park after Barrett was killed.

"What are you doing in town?" Donald asked her.

"I live pretty close. I stopped for a sandwich."

"It's a good place. Their sandwiches are great.

Listen, could you put in a good word for me about the dispatcher's job? I mean if you have the time, and you wouldn't mind."

Shelly blew out a breath. "I don't know if I can do that."

Donald looked like he'd been slapped.

Shelly stared into the young man's eyes. "Why did you lie to me about being in the park on the morning Mr. Barrett's body was found?"

Donald paled. "What? What do you mean?"

"You told me you weren't there."

"Why are you asking me about this?" Donald stammered.

"Because, I saw pictures from that morning. You are in one of them."

"Me? What picture? Who took the picture?"

"Look, Donald. You told me you weren't there, but clearly you were. I don't like being lied to. Why did you do it?"

"I...."

"So you were there?"

"I ... I don't remember. Maybe I was. I'd have to think about it."

Shelly rolled her eyes and climbed onto the bicycle. "Forget it." She left Donald on the sidewalk blinking after her.

As soon as she got home, she planned to call Jay to report Donald's lie. When she was a few blocks away from the sandwich shop, a wash of anxiety flooded her veins and a terrible thought raced through her mind, and for a second, she almost lost her balance.

What if Donald is the killer?

THE SUN WAS SETTING and the shadows of the trees were long and dark when Shelly pulled the bike into her driveway. She was sorry to see that Juliet's car wasn't in the driveway next door because she wanted to talk over what had happened in town and discuss her worries that Donald Chapel could be Barrett's killer.

Donald lied about his presence in the park. Had he returned that morning to watch the discovery of the body? Wilson Barrett showed up in the high school parking lot when Donald was menacing Pam McFee over the dent and the scratches he'd caused to her vehicle. Was Donald resentful about Barrett's interference? Donald had a temper. Did his resentment slowly grow into rage? The young man's obsession with law enforcement seemed slightly odd. The landlord's wife had seen Donald pacing around his apartment at all hours of the night.

Shelly's muscles felt weak with worry. All she wanted to do was to forget the case, go inside, see Justice, change clothes, and get comfortable on the sofa.

When she climbed the porch steps to the front door, she heard Justice howling and saw her in the bedroom window, her little paws on the glass and her tail twitching wildly.

Shelly's body filled with dread as she pulled out her key to rush inside and see what was tormenting the Calico.

Hurrying into the living room, she stopped in her tracks.

Tina Barrett stood near the fireplace, her eyes blazing with hatred.

Shelly clutched her key ring. She would use it as a weapon if Tina came at her. She only hoped the woman didn't have a gun.

"This is my house," Shelly growled.

Justice flew into the room and leapt onto the sofa table, hissing and spitting at the auburn-haired woman.

Tina yelled at the cat and took two steps towards the animal.

"Run, Justice," Shelly urged the cat and the feline jumped down and snuck behind one of the chairs. Filled with rage, Shelly's eyes flashed at Tina. "If you touch that cat, it will be the last thing you ever lay your hands on."

Like an evil witch, Tina threw her head back and roared with laughter. "So tough. So indignant. Too bad it won't do you any good."

"How did it feel to murder someone you used to love?" Shelly asked.

"I wouldn't know since I'm not the one who murdered him."

"Mike Meeks."

"You're correct. Good job," Tina mocked Shelly.

"But you certainly had a hand in it."

"Think what you want." A little smile showed on the woman's mouth.

"Where's Mike now?"

"He took a little trip."

"How did you know you were still Wilson's bene-ficiary?" Shelly asked.

Tina sighed. "You and that cop didn't figure that out? Mike was Wilson's financial advisor for years and years. Once every five to ten years, Mike asks his clients to bring in all important documents, wills, investment statements, bank statements, any health care proxies or powers of attorney. Mike reviews them and explains which ones need to be updated." Her smile grew wider. "About six months ago, it was time for Wilson to have Mike review his important papers. Mike noticed I was still the beneficiary."

"So you and Mike had been dating for more than six months?"

"Don't call it dating. We saw each other once in a while. When Mike told me I was still in Wilson's will, it was time for me to up my interest in Mike. He's having financial difficulties so I may have suggested we do something to get Wilson's money. I have no intention of sharing it with Mikey, of course, but he doesn't know that."

"You were also seeing Clay Daniels."

"That's right." Tina's eyes narrowed.

"Why did you kill him? Had he put you in his will, too?" Shelly needled the woman.

"That was all Mike. He found out I was seeing Clay and decided to end my affair with him by ending Clay's life." Tina's expression was as hard as nails. "That was a mistake. One that will end Mike's life ... very soon."

"Lewis from the sandwich shop is your friend?" Shelly questioned, trying to buy time.

"Ha. My *friend*." Tina spit the words out. "The

man likes money and will do what is asked of him when he is well paid."

Shelly could see Justice slinking out from behind the chair, her eyes pinned on Tina. If the Calico made a move to attack the intruder, Shelly would take her chance to defend herself.

Tina reached into her pocket and removed something. A taser.

Shelly's stomach lurched. If she was touched by the taser, she wouldn't be able to fight back.

If Tina had a gun, she would have taken it out by now. Shelly weighed her options. She could make a run for the door. She might be able to outrun the woman. It was her best chance.

Shelly whirled around and bolted for the front door. Tina was a second behind.

Before Shelly could cross the room, the door flew open and a man charged in like a linebacker ready to take out an opponent.

Before Tina could react, the man plowed into her and sent her flying through the air before she landed in a heap, unconscious, her taser skidding over the wood floor.

Justice let out a wild hiss as she took a position standing right next to the woman.

"Donald." Shelly was so shaken and overcome

she could barely squeeze the word from her throat. "How did you know?"

Standing over Tina with his hands formed into fists, Donald Chapel noticed the section of pipe on the floor near the fireplace that Tina planned to use on Shelly after she'd disabled her with the taser.

"I *didn't* know. I came to tell you why I lied about being in the park. I didn't want you to think I was the killer. I didn't want you to think I was bad." Donald's round cheeks were bright red. "I saw you and Tina through the window. The front door was partly open. I could hear what she was saying to you. I was waiting for the right moment to rush in."

Shelly walked over to the man and wrapped her arms around him. Several tears fell from her eyes onto his shoulder. "Thank you, Donald. You saved my life."

Justice trilled from her spot on the floor keeping her gaze glued to the still unconscious Tina Barrett.

25

"I always miss all the exciting stuff." Juliet placed a platter of cut-up vegetables on the long picnic table in Shelly's backyard. Little strings of white lights were strung between the branches of the trees.

"You're welcome to handle the exciting stuff from now on." Shelly smiled at the man sitting across from her. "Unless Donald agrees to be my permanent bodyguard."

Donald chuckled. "I'll have to think about that. I like my job at the dispatch."

Friends and family had gathered in Shelly's yard for a cookout to celebrate finding the killer responsible for the murders of Wilson Barrett and Mayor Clay Daniels.

Earlier in the day, Shelly, Jay, and Juliet had discussed the dreams. Shelly told them, "My dreams of the pictures floating on the air must have symbolized the photos from social media showing Donald in the park ... and Lauren touching her stomach and her head must have been indicating to me that Mr. Barrett got tased in the stomach before Meeks hit him in the back of the skull. In one dream, Lauren kept looking into the woods. I must have suspected that someone had hidden in the woods and ambushed Mr. Barrett."

Shelly had cleared her throat and went on. "If Juliet hadn't shown me the picture of Donald from social media, I wouldn't have confronted him about his lie of not being in the park when I ran into him outside the sandwich shop. And if I hadn't confronted him, Donald wouldn't have come to my house to explain himself. That photo from social media played a part in Donald saving my life."

Over in Juliet's connecting yard, Jack, Andrew, Jay's husband, Eddie, Dwayne from Glad Hill Farm, and Henry from the diner were playing a competitive game of horseshoes with shouts and cheers punctuating the air every few minutes. Justice sat on the fence watching the men play their rousing game.

"Mike Meeks was picked up in New York City,"

Jay informed the people around the picnic table. "Tina had sent him there to wait until the will was probated. She told him once she had the money, they would leave the country together. Tina never intended to do such a thing. Tina and Mike have been busy in jail accusing each other of being the killer. She called him an idiot and a lackey. She told us Meeks was the one who orchestrated the killings. He was the one responsible. She had nothing to do with it. Of course, she's lying."

"Meeks denies everything?" Melody, from the diner, asked.

"Mr. Meeks might be cutting a deal with the district attorney's office. What we believe from interviewing both Tina and Mike is that Tina was the mastermind. When Mike told her she was still in Barrett's will, she concocted the idea to use Mike. She would pretend to be in love with him, have Mike kill Barrett, and then inherit the money. Once she had the inheritance, she would rat out Mike claiming he was the one who tried to get her involved and that he was the one who was the killer."

"Donald," Andrew called from the horseshoe game. "Come help me. I need someone good on my team."

Donald nodded and held up a finger to indicate he would be right there.

Jay continued, "Mike Meeks murdered Mayor Daniels because Tina was having an affair with him. Tina was enraged, but she kept it together so she wouldn't be implicated in Barrett's murder. She told Mike to go to New York on the pretense he was looking for investors for his company. She wanted him out of her hair. He was too much of a liability."

"Did Tina take part in the murder?" Melody asked.

Jay sadly nodded her head. "Tina knew Mr. Barrett's routine. She hurried to the park to intercept him on his walk home. She pretended she wanted him to help out Mike Meeks, but she really wanted to walk with him until they reached the crest of the hill. Once they got there, she tased him in the abdomen. Mike Meeks was hiding in the woods. He rushed out and beat Mr. Barrett to death, then he and Tina made their escape through the woods."

"What terrible, terrible monsters," Juliet said. "Obviously, the blood found on that rag in the trunk of David Pillman's car wasn't Wilson Barrett's blood."

"The blood tested as a match to Pillman's friend," Jay told them. "Pillman was telling the truth about the flat tire and his friend accidentally hitting himself in the face with the tire iron. Pillman was no prize of a human being. He hated Mr. Barrett and was delighted that he'd met such an awful fate."

Shelly poured glasses of lemonade for everyone. "The delivery guy had been paid by Tina to lie about the time he delivered the food to her on the evening Barrett was killed. After I talked to him, he called Tina to alert her to my inquiries. Tina believed I thought she was the killer so she went to my house and waited for me."

Juliet glanced over at Donald. "But someone saved the day."

With red cheeks, Donald smiled. "I was upset that Shelly was angry with me. I told her I wasn't at the park the morning the body was found because I worried she would think I was the killer, or that I was weird for standing around looking at the dead body. I was watching the crowd looking for anyone suspicious. I've read that sometimes killers show up again to the crime scene to watch what's going on. I was afraid when Jay found out I had that fit in the parking lot of the high school, she wouldn't ever hire me for anything at the police station."

"We understand why you were upset that day in the lot," Jay said. "You were afraid your insurance would be canceled and you'd have no way to get to work. Since the incident in the parking lot, Donald's been going to counseling to learn to deal with his emotions."

"I want to do better," Donald said. "I want to understand and control my feelings. I'm learning a lot with my counselor. My parents died in an accident right before I turned eighteen. I have a lot of pent up feelings about loss and grief. It's good to be able to talk to someone about them."

"We're proud of you," Jay told the man.

The men walked over to join the others at the table for the cold drinks and snacks.

"We're playing again after a ten-minute break," Jack told Donald. "We need your help."

"How about we play the men against the women?" Jay suggested to whoops of agreement from the other females.

"Bring it on," Andrew playfully taunted them. "Now we really need Donald on our side."

Shelly and Juliet brought out mini pizzas, small meat and vegetable turnovers, and some cupcakes.

"If we're going to have a competitive game of horseshoes," Juliet said, "then we all need our strength, so eat up, everyone."

Shelly reached for one of the mini pizzas. "And

after horseshoes, we challenge you men to a game of cornhole."

Jack put his arm around his girlfriend. "Before we play, Shelly has some good news to share."

Everyone's attention turned to the young woman. Justice jumped up on the picnic bench and rubbed her head against Shelly's leg.

Shelly patted the cat and chuckled. "Justice and I have made a decision about how to spend our money."

"What have you decided to do?" Juliet looked to her friend with an eager expression.

"This house means a lot to us. It's the prefect size and location in town, but most important of all, it's right next door to our best friend." Shelly smiled and made eye contact with Juliet. "I wouldn't want to live anywhere else so I'm taking up the landlord's offer. Pam McFee told me I'm approved for a mortgage. I'm buying the bungalow."

Juliet whooped and the others clapped and cheered.

Shelly hugged her friend and accepted congratulations from everyone.

"You can always save up again to have a bakery someday," Juliet said.

Taking a look at Henry, Melody, and Dwayne,

Shelly said, "The bakery might not happen for a very long time, if at all. If I open a bakery, I'd miss my seeing my friends every day." Shelly looked at each of the people who had gathered in her yard. "I feel like the luckiest person in the world."

"Okay," Andrew said, "enough of sunshine and love. Men, put on your A-game. It's time to win this challenge." And turning around, he led the exuberant group of friends ... and one lovely Calico cat ... back over to the horseshoes pit to begin the great battle.

THANK YOU FOR READING!

Books by J.A. WHITING can be found here:
www.amazon.com/author/jawhiting

To hear about new books and book sales, please sign up for my mailing list at:
www.jawhitingbooks.com

Your email will never be sold, shared, or spammed.

If you enjoyed the book, please consider leaving a review. A few words are all that's needed. It would be very much appreciated.

ALSO BY J.A. WHITING

OLIVIA MILLER MYSTERIES (not cozy)

SWEET COVE COZY MYSTERIES

LIN COFFIN COZY MYSTERIES

CLAIRE ROLLINS COZY MYSTERIES

PAXTON PARK COZY MYSTERIES

SEEING COLORS MYSTERIES

ABOUT THE AUTHOR

J.A. Whiting lives with her family in Massachusetts. Whiting loves reading and writing mystery and suspense stories.

Visit / follow me at:
www.jawhitingbooks.com
www.bookbub.com/authors/j-a-whiting
www.amazon.com/author/jawhiting
www.facebook.com/jawhitingauthor

23043321R00156

Printed in Great Britain
by Amazon